MK888

A MEDICAL EXPERIMENT LIKE NO OTHER

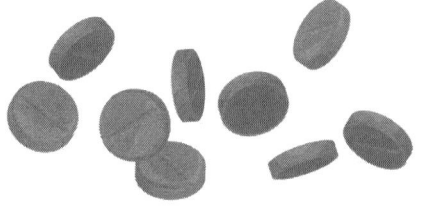

Stephen Ball

Copyright © Stephen Ball 2022
This book is sold subject to the condition that it shall not, by way of trade or otherwise, be lent, resold, hired out, or otherwise circulated without the publisher's prior consent in any form of binding or cover other than that in which it is published and without a similar condition including this condition being imposed on the subsequent publisher.
The moral right of Stephen Ball has been asserted.
ISBN: 9798838841643

This is a work of fiction. Names, characters, businesses, organizations, places, events and incidents either are the product of the author's imagination or are used fictitiously. Any resemblance to actual persons, living or dead, events, or locales is entirely coincidental.

CONTENTS

INTRODUCTION 1
THE PATIENTS 2
MEDICAL TEAM 3
CHAPTER 1:   Day 1   Introductions 4
CHAPTER 2:   Day 2   Looking Ahead 10
CHAPTER 3:   Day 3   Review Of The Patients 14
CHAPTER 4:   Day 4   Barium Swallow Test 19
CHAPTER 5:   Day 5   Ph Testing 25
CHAPTER 6:   Day 6   The Library 30
CHAPTER 7:   Day 7   Electric Shock Test 36
CHAPTER 8:   Day 8   Week 1 Review 45
CHAPTER 9:   Day 9   Cancer, Oh My God 49
CHAPTER 10: Day 10   In The Laboratory 54
CHAPTER 11: Day 11   Losing Money 58
CHAPTER 12: Day 12   Ear Testing 65
CHAPTER 13: Day 13   Day Out At The Bird Park 82
CHAPTER 14: Day 14   Sudden Death 85
CHAPTER 15: Day 15   Week 2 Review 89
CHAPTER 16: Day 16   Ct Scans 94
CHAPTER 17: Day 17   Missing Patient 100
CHAPTER 18: Day 18   Food Intolerance Tests 106
CHAPTER 19: Day 19   Alcohol And Non-Alcohol Tests 121
CHAPTER 20: Day 20   The Return Of The Bad Man 127
CHAPTER 21: Day 21   Visiting Home 133
CHAPTER 22: Day 22   Week 3 Review 137
CHAPTER 23: Day 23   Legal Threat 142
CHAPTER 24: Day 24   Unpaid Bar Bill 146
CHAPTER 25: Day 25   Smoke Chamber Test 150
CHAPTER 26: Day 26   Music Test 160
CHAPTER 27: Day 27   Mk888 Drugs Robbery 166
CHAPTER 28: Day 28   Nose And Throat Examinations 172

CHAPTER 29: Day 29	Week 4 Review	185
CHAPTER 30: Day 30	Conclusion	190
ABOUT THE AUTHOR		200

INTRODUCTION

In the world today there are approximately 7.7 billion people. About a third, say two and a half billion, suffer from some form of coughing. Some mild, some severe, but practically all annoying. In this book, Professor Lee and his team of medical experts carry out a medical experiment using a new drug called MK888. The drug, combined with routine medical testing and some bizarre new tests, result in one patient suffering from severe depression and another suffering a heart attack. Set in the city state of Singapore and conducted in a state-of-the-art ENT Hospital, the medical tests create an ebb and flow of excitement and mystery.

THE PATIENTS

SG1 Singaporean male, 45 years old – Factory Worker
SG2 Singaporean female, 33 years old – Accountant
SG3 Singaporean male, 20 years old – Art Student
SG4 Singaporean female, 48 years old – Lawyer
SG5 Singaporean male, 71 years old – Retired Teacher
ML1 Malaysian male, 60 years old – Restaurant Owner
ML2 Malaysian female, 24 years old – Fashion Model
HK1 Hong Kong male, 36 years old – Professional Gambler
GB1 British female, 29 years old – Business Owner
TW1 Taiwanese female, 21 years old – Student (Business)

MEDICAL TEAM

Professor Benjamin Lee, male, 52 years old, Singaporean
Dr Fu Su Wong, male, 38 years old, Singaporean
Dr Audrey Tan, female, 37 years old, Singaporean
Dr Aneleise Malinowski, female, 41 years old, Russian
Nurse Asterina Cheng, female, 25 years old, Singaporean

CHAPTER 1

DAY ONE

INTRODUCTIONS

SINGAPORE ENT HOSPITAL (SPECIAL WING) 2019

Professor Benjamin Lee entered the meeting room followed by Dr Fu Su Wong, Nurse Asterina Cheng, and Dr Aneleise Malinowski. Dr Audrey Tan was already seated at the end of the large table. Greetings were exchanged.

'Our patients should all be here soon,' said Lee.

Dr Fu Su Wong adjusted the air conditioning to make the meeting room more comfortable. 'It's a bit cold,' said Dr Aneleise Malinowski.

After fifteen minutes all patients had arrived and were seated around the table.

'Welcome everybody,' said Lee. 'I hope all patients were able to check in to their rooms and found them comfortable?' Several nods of the head in agreement were received. Lee stood up and continued speaking. 'For today's meeting we will go around the table and introduce ourselves. Then me and my medical team will go through the plan for our 30-day experiment, beginning tomorrow, after assessing everyone.' Coughs were heard from the end of the table from HK1 and SG4.

'Ok then,' said Lee, 'I will be overall in charge of this experiment. I was born in Singapore in 1968. I have two brothers and one sister. After completing my education in Singapore, I attended medical school in California, USA. My speciality subject is throat disorders. After returning from California, I met my wife Mellissa, and we have one son and one daughter. I enjoy listening to classic music and Cantopop. I will now hand you over to Dr Fu Su Wong.'

Lee sat down and Fu Su Wong stood up. 'Welcome everybody,' he said with a smile. 'After the usual education here in Singapore, I became a student at a medical college with special interest in hearing loss and coughing problems. I was born in 1982 and am divorced with no children.'

Dr Fu Su Wong sat down, and Nurse Asterina Cheng stood up. 'Welcome everybody,' she said. 'I was born in Singapore in 1994. Both my parents were doctors, so I guess that is why I chose the medical route. My medical interest is in all ENT-related matters. I enjoy cooking Asian and Western food. I enjoy watching historical films.'

Nurse Asterina Cheng sat down, and Dr Audrey Tan stood up. 'Hello to everyone,' she said. 'I was born in 1982 and after school and university I studied at medical school in Singapore. Part of my studying involved a swop with a South Korean medical student. I spent two years studying in Seoul and this included studying a new Electric Shock Treatment Machine. I am interested in Art, particularly paintings of sceneries from around the world.'

Dr Audrey Tan sat down, and Dr Aneleise Malinowski stood up. 'Good morning to you all,' she said. 'I was born in Saint Petersburg, Russia, forty-one years ago. After university, where I studied International Law, I moved to Moscow to study medicine. My special interest is in new drug trials and nasal rebuilding. After qualifying in Moscow, I took the job here as Head of Laboratory services. Outside of working I enjoy watching TV comedies and going to the theatre for ballet or opera.'

Dr Aneleise Malinowski sat down, and Professor Lee stood up. Lee thanked his medical team for their introductions. 'Could I now ask that all patients introduce themselves in the same way as my colleagues have just done. Starting with SG1 please, thank you.'

Lee sat down just as the door opened. Two catering assistants entered the room with trays of coffee and placed them on the table and left the room.

'SG1,' said Lee. SG1 stood up.

'Hi everyone,' he said boldly. 'I am a forty-five-year-old Singaporean factory worker. My job involves making sure the assembly line is working correctly. My main interest is travelling to Japan and Taiwan which I have enjoyed immensely. I met my wife at school, and we got married at age twenty. My own coughing problem is very acute and has got worse in recent years.'

SG1 sat down and SG2 got up and sneezed. 'Excuse me,' she said. 'Hello everyone. I am SG2. My job is as an accountant in Singapore. I am thirty-three years old, single, and enjoy life apart from the bad dry cough which I have suffered from for about three years now.'

SG2 sat down and SG3 got up, coughed, and cleared his throat. He coughed a second time and said, 'Excuse me. I am SG3 and was born twenty years ago in Singapore. My situation is that I am an Art Student at Singapore University. I hope to get a job one day designing clothes and homeware. My cough started a year ago and it is on and off, with possible food-related problems. I am interested in getting tattoos but my parents are not approving at the moment,' he laughed loudly.

SG3 sat down and SG4 stood up.

'Hi everyone, I am SG4. I was born in Singapore some forty-eight years ago. After school my family and myself moved to Canada. I studied Law at Montreal University for five years and then I worked in a law firm in Vancouver for ten years. After such time, I returned to Singapore and started my own law firm specialising in joint venture business deals. I am divorced with one daughter aged twenty-four.'

SG4 sat down and SG5 got up.

'Hello everyone. I am SG5. I am a retired Geography teacher, and I am married with three children and two grandchildren. My cough is very bad and after twenty years I am really angry that I cannot get to the bottom of it! My interests are cooking, watching football and Chinese Opera.'

SG5 sat down and ML1 stood up.

'Hello all. I am ML1. I was born sixty years ago in KL, Malaysia. My early life was in KL, but I moved to JB around thirty years ago, when I inherited my parents' seafood restaurant. I am married to Jenny, and we have five children and eleven grandchildren. My cough is a pain! I've had it for thirty years or more. I also suffer from a snoring problem which is driving my wife mad.' Several laughs are heard from the other patients around the table.

ML1 sat down and ML2 stood up.

'Hi everyone, I am ML2 a twenty-four-year-old Malaysian fashion model. I was born in Penang – a holiday island – and moved to Kuala Lumpur at five years old. I recently started my career as a model. My work is mainly for international fashion magazines. My main interest in life is travelling. So far, I have been to Thailand, Taiwan, Australia, and France. Oh! And my main problem, a stubborn cough for the past six months.'

ML2 sat down and HK1 stood up. 'Hello people I am HK1. I was born in Hong Kong thirty-six years ago. You could say I have had a colourful life, or very colourful. My job is as a professional gambler. I bet successfully on horse racing and football. It's not a normal life, being up and down constantly like a yo-yo! I have been married three times and have five children. My particular cough has been around for ten or more years. I know I should give up smoking, but I don't seem able to do so.'

HK1 sat down and GB1 stood up.

'Hello I'm GB1. I have British parents but was born in Singapore twenty-nine years ago and have lived here all my life. After a number of years helping my father with his antiques business, I took over the business a few years ago. I am married to Patrick, a Singaporean national, and we have no kids yet. I am interested in yoga and Chinese Opera. My coughing started five years ago and think it may be food related but not sure about it.'

GB1 sat down and TW1 stood up.

'Hello everyone. I am TW1, a twenty-one-year-old Taiwanese born in our capital Taipei. Recently, I came to Singapore to study International Business. My father has a manufacturing business and wants me to join the firm in the future. We'll see about that.' She laughed coyly. 'My cough started a year ago and it feels like I have a blockage in my throat, but not all the time.'

TW1 sat down and Professor Lee stood up.

'Thank you, everybody, for the introductions. I wish all patients luck with our experiment. Can I ask, have all patients submitted their questionnaires? If not, could they do it today and leave them in reception. Don't forget to provide all details of current medication and any health issues in addition to coughing. All patients will start their medication of the new drug MK888 tonight. One hundred milligrams will be taken as a tablet this evening. All future days will be a fifty-milligrams tablet in the morning and a fifty-milligrams tablet in the evening. You are also free to do as you wish for the rest of the day. Can I ask that all patients refrain from all alcohol during this experiment? Also, any smoking should be kept to the minimum.

'Tomorrow, we will all meet at 10 a.m. and my medical team will give you the full plan of our experiment, including the tests you will have and any other help we can give. The hospital also has a library with all kinds of books, medical and otherwise. You are welcome to spend time in there. Does anyone have any questions?'

SG5 stood up quickly. 'I forgot to bring my cough mixture, can I get some from the hospital pharmacy?'

Professor Lee said, 'Yes, if you go with Nurse Cheng to Pharmacy, you will be able to get a bottle of cough mixture.' SG5 thanked Lee. 'See everyone tomorrow at 10 then.'

Everyone left the meeting room.

CHAPTER 2

DAY TWO
LOOKING AHEAD

10.00 a.m., meeting room. All medical staff were present but only half of the patients. The last two patients to arrive, SG3 and TW1, arrived at 10.15 and received a dirty look from Professor Lee as they walked into the room and sat down.

Professor Lee stood up and said, 'Good morning. In future please can you all try to arrive on time. Today we will be discussing the detailed plan for our experiment. In the world today there are approximately 7.7 billion people. Around a third, which is more than two and a half billion, suffer from coughing caused by numerous diseases. Some known, some not yet known. We face a huge task here. Our experiment with MK888 may take us to many roads of frustration. There may be no progress in reducing the problem for you, the participants. We may partly solve the problem or may get indication of another route to pursue in medication. You can be sure you are in the hands of an excellent team here. My team are all experts in the subject of ENT matters.'

HK1 coughed loudly, 'Excuse me.'

SG1 coughed loudly, 'Excuse me too.'

Professor Lee nodded and continued speaking. 'Some of the tests in our program will apply to all patients. Other tests will be selective to only a few patients, depending on their progress and suitability. We will be taking daily blood pressure checks and weekly blood sample tests.

'Special tests will be carried out and, where they have a high level of discomfort, we will ask sometimes for volunteers to participate in the test if it's controversial. You will be encouraged to keep a record of anything unusual in the way you feel. We don't know what to expect, we really don't. As a matter of interest, could we take a vote to see the number of people with a predominantly dry cough and the number of people who often cough with phlegm. So, could all patients who think their cough is a dry cough raise their hand now please?' A total of seven hands were raised. Professor Lee nodded appreciation. 'Ok, all the people who think they predominantly cough with mucus/phlegm raise their hands please?' Two hands were seen raised. 'Thank you,' said Lee. 'So that's nine responses. Who has not raised their hand?'

SG5 raised his hand and said, 'It's about fifty-fifty. I have been coughing for around twenty years. Sometimes I am coughing in the morning with phlegm. Other times it can be a dry cough. I think my body produces mucus if I eat anything with cream. If I eat an ice cream today, I will have a blocked nose tomorrow!'

Dr Fu Su Wong and Dr Audrey Tan looked at each other. Dr Fu Su Wong asked SG5, 'Have you ever had food allergy tests?'

'No,' replied SG5. 'I may have a dairy problem as I like Indian food, and this seems to make me cough and suffer from mucus production thereafter.'

'Interesting,' said Lee. 'Thanks everyone. There will be some emphasis on the type of cough in this experiment. The result just now was what I expected. More people have a dry cough than a wet one! The people coughing phlegm tend to be older people. Smokers are more prone to phlegm coughs than non-smokers. I just need to disappear somewhere for a while to attend to something. Audrey, could you take over while I am absent? Please go through some of the testing we are planning.'

Audrey Tan nodded, 'No problem.' Audrey stood up and Lee left the meeting room. Minor coughs were heard coming from SG1, SG5, and ML1. A severe coughing fit started with HK1 which lasted a minute and a half. Audrey looked concerned. 'I'll get some more water,' she said. Audrey picked up the phone on the table and phoned the kitchen. 'Hello, it's Dr Tan. Can you bring two bottles of water to the meeting room? Thanks.' Audrey put the phone down.

'Ok so let's go through some of the forthcoming tests you will be having. Starting with the ear then. We will ask if you can have any ear-related problems. Deafness, tinnitus, and ear discharge. Any injuries to the ear. Any exposure to extreme noise. The inspection of the ear will take place after wax removal. We will carry out ear inspections of the pinna. The pinna is the outer ear area. We will look for any abnormalities in the size and shape and check to see if there are lesions present. We will then move on to the inner ear and inspect the ear drum. Also, we will carry out some basic hearing tests.'

Audrey stopped and had a sip of water. 'There is the Webers Fork Test. A vibrating fork is placed in your hand, and you will be asked if you can hear anything. We will ask if you can hear from both ears and, if so, is the sound equal in both ears. There is another test called The Rinnies Test which is a bit more complicated, so I won't go in to that now. We will carry out a music test, you will listen to a piece of music and then be asked to name as many instruments as possible.

'Moving on to the nose examinations. Common symptoms of nasal conditions are airways obstruction, runny nose, sneezing, loss of smell, sinusitis, snoring. Some of the issues covered include allergies, smoking, pets at home, trauma, general medication. We will inspect the nose size and shape. Look for any redness, discharge, or crusts. We will analyse both sides for unequal airways through breathing exercises, such as sniffing from each nostril while the other is closed. Nasal endoscopy tests will be conducted, among others.

'Moving on to the throat, we will want to know the history of the patients' use of alcohol and tobacco. A history of dental work will be useful as well. The mouth will be looked at closely and the tongue for anything unusual. Cheeks and gums will be examined for any redness and signs of legions.' Audrey took a sip of water and asked if anyone had any questions.

ML2 stood up. 'What time will we start the tests on day four?'

'About 10 in the morning. If it changes, there will be a message on the computer in your rooms. You are basically free for tomorrow, day three. Nurse Cheng will take your blood pressure at some time. If there's no more questions, I will declare the meeting closed.' Everybody left the meeting room.

CHAPTER 3

DAY THREE
REVIEW OF THE PATIENTS

Professor Lee walked into his office, he shook his umbrella to get rid of the rain drops he had just endured. He sat down at his desk and turned on the computer. The phone rang. Lee picked it up. 'Hello, Professor Lee.' After half a minute listening to the caller, Lee replied, 'That patient was at the hospital about five years ago. I don't remember the operation details but will check the file and get back to you. Ok. Bye.' Lee put the phone down, carried on logging in to his computer, and read his emails.

Dr Fu Su Wong knocked on Lee's door and entered. Lee turned around to look at him. They exchanged hellos. Wong said, 'I will have all the patients' records ready in the meeting room in fifteen minutes.'

'That's good. I think it will be very interesting.'

Wong said, 'Aneleise will not be joining us today. She is working on some test kits concerning MK888 on mice.'

'Ok, I will see you shortly in the meeting room,' Lee replied. Wong left the office and Lee returned to his emails.

In the meeting room Audrey Tan and Asterina Cheng were seated ready for the meeting. They were browsing through the patients' files. Tan looked at Cheng and smiled. 'Where do you live?'

Cheng replied, 'I have a small condo in Woodlands. It's

good for the occasional visit to Malaysia. And you?'

'I am living in East Coast Parkway. I like being by the sea. In our condo we can leave the windows open at night and not have the air con on.'

'And you have a lot of nice seafood restaurants in that area, right?' Cheng remarked.

'Yes, that's right,' said Tan.

Dr Fu Su Wong entered the meeting room. 'Hi both,' he said. Cheng and Wong both greeted the latest arrival. Wong sat down and picked up a file, he opened it and started reading. He flicked over a few sheets and then spoke. 'Coughing up blood is a tricky one. It can be nothing more than the high stress of coughing frequently. Or something more sinister!'

Professor Lee sat down and said, 'So, who are we looking at first?' Wong reached across and took the first medical folder and opened it.

Wong smiled and said, 'HK1. Our Hong Kong patient.'

'The one with the bad habits,' added Cheng.

Wong read from the file. 'HK1 is a 36-year-old professional gambler, interesting, a smoker of 20 cigarettes a day, and a drinker of American whiskey. His cough is quite acute, often with phlegm.'

Lee said, 'The cough is a concern. In a patient of this age, you would not expect to see a really bad cough. In our lifestyle recommendations we will advise a stop-smoking program.' Wong closed the file and put it to one side.

Wong took the next file from the top of the pile and opened it. He looked at a couple of pages and then said, 'Ok next is SG4. A Singaporean female aged 48 years old. Medical history appears ok apart from an acute cough. The cough has been combined with haemoptysis on two occasions.'

Audrey Tan commented, 'As it was only two instances of coughing blood it probably isn't serious.'

'SG4 is a heavy smoker and has suffered with a bad cough for about four years,' Wong added.

Lee said, 'Ok, next patient.' Wong took the next medical file and opened it.

'Ok we now have ML1, a Malaysian male aged 60 years old. Has a seafood business in JB. He is an ex-smoker. According to the notes in his file, he gave up smoking 10 years ago after being a moderate smoker for 30 years. His cough also goes back 30 years.'

Audrey Tan remarked, 'Well after 10 years quitting smoking, he should be free of nicotine.'

Professor Lee gave his opinion. 'I'm not sure about that 10-year theory. Anything else interesting in his file?'

Wong shuffled the papers. 'Not really. A minor operation for sinusitis and an operation to deal with a fistula ulcer.' Wong closed the file and placed it neatly on the read pile. He then pushed the unread pile towards Nurse Cheng. 'Could you do some of the reviews?'

Cheng picked up the file on top and opened it. After a quick flick of the enclosures, she said, 'Right now we are reviewing our youngest patient. SG3 is a 20-year-old art student with a mild cough, which began a year ago. Only thing of interest is a pain in the right ear. Possible cause is listening to music too loud via portable earphones.'

Lee commented, 'Ok we'll keep that problem in memory when we come to test the patient.' Cheng closed the file and placed it on the read pile.

She picked up the next file and opened it. 'Here we have SG1, a 45-year-old Singaporean male factory worker.

According to the file the patient suffers from high blood pressure but is taking medication. 50 mg a day of Melatroxodine. Another ailment is haemorrhoids. The condition has been banded without success. Ointments and suppositories have helped reduce the discomfort. The cough of this patient goes back some twenty years.'

Lee commented, 'That's a long time to be suffering. It might be lifestyle rather than something serious.' Cheng closed the file and moved on to the next.

'Right, next is SG2, a 33-year-old Singaporean national. An accountant with a three-year coughing problem. Only point of interest is an abortion at the age of 18.'

'Do we know at what stage the abortion took place?'

Cheng read the notes and said, 'It was at the three-month stage.' Wong asked if the patient had any subsequent pregnancies. Cheng looked in the file. 'Nothing on file to indicate that.' Cheng turned to Audrey Tan and said, 'Would you like to do the last few?'

'OK.'

Tan opened the next file. 'Here we have SG5, a Singaporean male Geography teacher. Has been coughing since he had a car accident 20 years ago.'

Wong said, 'I wouldn't have thought there was a connection, what were the injuries?'

Tan studied the file and said, 'Broken back, whiplash injuries. Physiotherapy for 18 months. Recently getting pain in both hips and awaiting a hip replacement operation.'

Lee smiled at Tan and said, 'Next.'

Tan opened the next file and shuffled the papers. She cleared her throat and then said, 'Ok next patient is ML2, a Malaysian female aged 24 years old. Her job is a fashion model. She has suffered a bad cough for six months. Usual medicines have not helped.' Tan laughed quietly. 'Something interesting here. Two bouts of Venereal disease. Chlamydia in 2016 and Gonorrhoea in 2017. If ML2 had oral sex, then the Gonorrhoea may have caused the cough! Interesting. We'll investigate further.' Tan closed the file quickly and placed it neatly on the read pile.

'Ok next we have GB1,' said Tan. 'A British female aged 29. Born in Singapore to antique-shop-owning parents. On the file we have a couple of things. Irregular periods since puberty. And food poisoning, actually two lots of food poisoning. One was quite recent. Apparently, after eating an oyster omelette at the Newton Hawker centre. The coughing problem goes back about five years.'

Lee commented, 'I don't know of any food poisoning links to permanent coughs, but we'll keep that information to hand.' Tan closed the file.

Tan opened the final patient file. 'Ok so our final patient is a 21-year-old Taiwanese female. Currently lives in Singapore and a student at the University of Singapore studying International Business. TW1 has been coughing regularly for about one year. She said that sometimes it feels like a blockage in the throat. Previous medical tests have not found anything.'

Wong said, 'Well tomorrow we are conducting the Barium Swallow Test so that might tell us more about Miss Taiwan.'

Lee stood up. 'Must get on. Tomorrow will be busy.' Everybody followed Lee out of the meeting room.

CHAPTER 4

DAY FOUR
BARIUM SWALLOW TEST

The treatment room looked neat and tidy. Dr Fu Su Wong and Nurse Asterina Cheng checked the various medicines prior to the day's testing.

'What's the first test today?' Cheng enquired.

'The Barium Swallow Test, then the basic Hearing Test, and then the Internal Ear,' Wong replied.

The clock in the corner of the treatment room buzzed. Wong and Cheng looked at it to see it was 10 a.m. Cheng walked over to the worktop containing the colour solution to be used in the swallow test. She counted the beakers that were stacked up. There were exactly 10. She nodded at the beakers in satisfaction.

At 10.15 there was a knock on the door. 'Come in,' said Wong. A girl from reception entered and handed Wong a brown folder. 'This is the first patient, SG1' she said. Wong thanked her and she left the room. Wong studied the file briefly and then went out of the treatment room and looked left to the patient seating area. 'SG1,' he said loudly. SG1 got up and followed Wong, carrying a basket with ~~her~~ his clothes. His blue medical gown hung loosely over his body. Cheng welcomed SG1 and asked him to sit on the upper end of the treatment bed. Cheng took the medical folder from Wong and turned to SG1 and said, 'Ok we will ask you to take a drink and swallow it in various positions. Standing up, sitting down, lying down on your side. The drink will taste a little unpleasant and you may suffer from constipation and stomach-ache the next day.'

SG1 nodded, 'Ok.'

Wong continued, 'After the swallow test you will have a series of X-rays while you're inside is coated with the liquid.'

SG1 sat up with his back straight on the end of the bed as Cheng handed him the beaker and said, 'Drink a mouthful and swallow it as if you were having a normal drink.' SG1 followed the instructions and then coughed slightly.

'It's not a nice taste,' he said. Wong stood a few metres away, observing the test.

Cheng smiled at SG1 and said, 'When you are ready lay down on the bed and take another mouthful of the barium liquid and swallow it.' SG1 coughed lightly and then took the barium and swallowed. Cheng told SG1 to have a little rest and then, for the third and final test, for him to lay on his side while drinking. SG1 followed instructions and handed the beaker to Cheng.

'How do you feel?' Wong asked.

'Not too bad. It's an unusual taste!'

Wong said, 'Just give yourself a few moments to recover and then Nurse Cheng will take you to the X-ray department.' Cheng took SG1 down to the X-ray department waiting area. They exchanged goodbyes.

Cheng returned to the treatment room, Wong was talking on his mobile phone. 'We tried that with a patient before and it didn't work. Yes, maybe. Ok, well good luck with that. Bye.' There was a knock on the door and then it slowly opened. A receptionist handed Wong the next patient's folder. Wong took the folder and said, 'Thanks, Melissa.' Wong looked over to where Cheng was standing and said, 'Next patient is the crazy one! SG3, the 20-year-old art student. How many colours are in his hair?'

Cheng chuckled, 'I don't know. Let's go and get him.' Cheng opened the door and looked at the patient waiting area. 'SG3 please,' she asked loudly. SG3 arose with his multi-coloured hair flapping on his shoulders. Cheng asked. 'Are you alright?'

'Yes,' he replied. They entered the treatment room together. Cheng pointed to the treatment bed and asked SG3 to sit there. Wong welcomed SG3 with a smile. Cheng filled a beaker with barium and handed it to SG3. 'Drink a mouthful please, while you are sitting normal,' she said. 'Just swallow it as if it was a normal drink.'

SG3 followed the instruction and when he had finished, he said, 'It tastes a bit like chalk, but not too bad. What is this test for?'

Wong said, 'It is to check if you can swallow normally and to see if any abnormalities are present.'

Cheng instructed SG3 to take another mouthful of barium while laying on his back. SG3 repositioned himself and downed the drink. 'Are you alright?' asked Cheng.

'Fine,' replied SG3.

'There is one more to do,' said Cheng. 'Lying on your side, take a mouthful and swallow.' SG3 switched to his side and took a mouthful. After which he coughed slightly. 'Ok good,' said Cheng. 'You may now sit up for a moment and then I'll take you down to X-ray.' After a couple of minutes Cheng beckoned SG3 from the seat. 'Let's go.'

Cheng and SG3 left the treatment room and walked to the

X-ray waiting room area. As Cheng made her way back, she noticed SG5 was waiting for his Barium Test. 'Come on in,' she said. 'Take a seat on the treatment bed.' SG5 gave Cheng his brown medical folder and sat down.

Wong looked at SG5 and said, 'How is your cough?'

'Not brilliant,' SG5 replied. 'I still have three to four bad coughing fits a day.'

'Really?' Wong responded. Cheng filled a beaker with barium and handed it to SG5.

'Drink this slowly,' she said. 'After that there will be two more times, one laying on your back and the other laying on your side.'

'No problem,' said SG5. He drank the barium while sitting on the treatment bed. 'Strange taste, and very salty,' said SG5.

'That's what most people say,' said Wong. The next two drinks went ok, as per the previous patients' experiences.

Meanwhile, in another treatment room, Audrey Tan was doing Ear Tests. HK1 was sitting in the treatment chair coughing loudly. 'Are you ok?' said Tan.

'Yes, fine thank you,' replied HK1. Tan fixed the cone-like gadget to the left ear of HK1 and secured it with wrap-round strings. Tan informed HK1 of what was coming. 'I will shoot a fast jet of water straight against the eardrum. It will feel a little strange, but it shouldn't feel too painful.'

'I had this procedure done once before as a young adult after a build up of a lot of wax in this ear,' said HK1. Tan handed HK1 a cushion.

'Hold on to this during the procedure.' HK1 thanked her.

'Ok here we go,' Tan said loudly, holding the ear wax removal gun to HK1'S ear. She pulled back the gun-like catch. Water gushed into the ear and out again. Tan's waterproof clothing got soaked. 'One more,' said Tan. She pulled the trigger again and held it for five seconds before releasing. Tan put the device down and dried herself with a towel. She handed another towel to HK1. 'How's it feel?' Tan asked.

'It feels a bit sensitive, but your voice is louder,' replied HK1.

Tan commented, 'That's the usual response.' Tan carried out the same procedure with the other ear and HK1 thanked her for cleaning the wax out.

Tan tidied up the mess and prepared for the next patient. Ten minutes later TW1 was in position to have her ears flushed. Tan said, 'How are you?'

'Well, I am suffering from a cough and feels like I have a small blockage,' replied TW1.

Tan inquired, 'Do you have a problem swallowing food?'

'No not at all,' said TW1.

'Probably only mucus,' said Tan. 'Have you ever had problems with your ears?' asked Tan.

'I had a bit of wax in the right ear, previously,' said TW1.

Tan said, 'Ok let's have a look at each ear.' Tan inspected each ear thoroughly and put the inspection device down on the worktop. 'There appears to be a little wax in the right ear, so we'll flush that out, no problem.' Tan applied the cone-shaped device to the right ear of the patient. She secured it tightly. 'Now this shouldn't be too uncomfortable.'

'Ok,' said TW1. Tan lifted up the spray gun and pointed it inside TW1's ear and pulled the trigger. The squirting of the liquid lasted all of ten seconds. Tan inspected the ear of the patient. 'We'll do it one more time, is that alright?' TW1 nodded. Tan carried out a second flushing and thanked the patient.

The next patient arrived in the treatment room with a tickly cough. GB1 apologised for the coughing fit. 'No problem,' said Tan. 'How are your ears, any problems?'

'Nothing I can think of,' said GB1.

'Let's take a look then,' said Tan. Tan looked at each ear in turn. 'Looks pretty free of wax, so I think it won't be necessary for flushing today.'

'That's great,' replied GB1. 'Will there be other tests?'

Tan replied, 'Quite likely in the time of this experiment. Maybe a sound test for everyone.' GB1 thanked Tan and left the Treatment Room.

CHAPTER 5

DAY FIVE
PH TESTING

Day five started with Professor Lee reading his emails and drinking coffee. He picked up the phone and dialled the number of Nurse Cheng. 'Asterina, I will be with you today on the 24ph Test,' he listened to her acknowledgment then continued. 'The two patients are ML1 and ML2. Okay see you in a bit.' Lee put the phone down and returned to his emails.

The clock struck 10 a.m. Lee shuffled papers on his desk, got up, then walked quickly out of his office and down to the treatment room. Nurse Cheng heard his footsteps coming and opened the door before he could. 'Good morning,' said Lee.

'Good morning,' said Cheng. 'ML1 is delayed so we will deal with ML2 first.'

'No problem,' said Lee.

Cheng opened a cupboard door and took out a PH testing kit. He removed the plastic wrapping and inspected the contents carefully. Cheng turned to Lee and said, 'Could you just check it over?'

'Sure,' said Lee, examining the gadget that would be fixed to ML2 for 24 hours. A knock on the door sounded. Cheng opened it and took the patient files for ML1 and ML2 from the receptionist. Cheng read the enclosed documents of the file from ML2 and then handed it to Lee for him to review. 'ML2 has suffered from food regurgitation so sounds like an acid problem,' said Lee.

'Yes, and the problem seems to have arrived at the same time as the bad cough,' added Cheng.

Cheng opened the door and peered over to look at the patient waiting area. 'ML2?' she enquired. ML2 got up from her seat and threw the magazine she was reading on to the chair and followed Cheng into the treatment room. Lee smiled and said, 'Hello,' gazing at her smart appearance. Cheng certainly noticed her colleague's interest in the patient's body.

Cheng pointed to the treatment bed and said, 'Please lay down and make yourself comfortable.' ML2 laid on the treatment bed and pulled her short skirt downwards in order to not reveal her underwear to Lee, who was still gazing intensely.

Lee walked over to the chair near the treatment bed and smiled widely at ML2. 'Right,' he said. 'I will just tell you what the PH24hr is and what it might tell us. We will shortly insert a long tube into your nose. Don't worry, we will numb the nose first. The tube will go down to your throat and then into your stomach. The tube is connected to a catheter box which will record various activities of the stomach. The tube will stay in your stomach for a period of 24 hours.'

'Will I be able to eat and drink in this period?' asked ML2.

'Yes,' replied Lee. 'You should have no problems, it will be slightly uncomfortable but bearable.'

'That's good,' said ML2. Cheng handed Lee the spray anaesthetic to put in the patient's nose. 'Okay just relax,' said Lee, trying to comfort the patient. Lee tested the device by spraying gently into the air away from them. He then turned to face ML2 and inserted the canister into her nose and sprayed twice. 'Okay we'll just let that take effect,' said Lee.

Ml2 sneezed gently. 'Sorry,' she said.

'Don't worry,' Lee said. Cheng took the spray canister from Lee and gave him the PH24 box and tube.

Lee looked at it closely and made sure the tube was inserted into the catheter box. 'Is the nose numb?' asked Lee. ML2 confirmed.

Lee held the box up to ML2. 'Okay, you will be attached to this box for 24 hours. The tube will be placed through your nose, all the way into your stomach. In the period of this test, can you press the button 'Start Food' just before you eat something? Then press the button 'Finish Food' when you have finished a meal.' ML2 nodded in agreement. Lee confirmed. 'Also, you will see a button that reads 'Discomfort'. You need to press that any time you feel a problem, like heartburn, indigestion, or anything that feels a little strange. When you come back tomorrow the device will be disconnected and the catheter box will be read by the computer, to see if you have any evidence of acid reflux.'

ML2 blinked several times and turned to Lee. 'It feels quite numb in the nose now.' Lee placed the catheter box on ML2's tummy and with the other hand took the tube to her left nostril and carefully inserted it inch by inch until it was all the way to the stomach. Lee asked, 'How does that feel?'

'Not great,' replied ML2.

'Don't worry' Lee said, trying to comfort her. 'It will just feel awkward, but you should still be able to go about your daily routine.' ML2 stood up and placed the catheter box in her bag and then put the bag over her shoulder.

'See you tomorrow then,' she said, walking out. Cheng and Lee said goodbye.

Lee looked at the next patient's file 'ML1 is interesting,' he said.

Cheng stood against the worktop with her arms folded. 'Why's that?' she questioned.

Lee answered, 'Well he's had a cough for 30 years and is a bad snorer.'

'I bet he's a smoker or ex-smoker' said Cheng. Lee shuffled the papers and then read from the medical notes. 'Smoked from age 20 to age 50. So, thirty years. Now 10 years without smoking.'

'Does that mean he is clear of all nicotine substances?' asked Cheng.

'I wouldn't like to say for certain. Medical opinion has differed on the ability of the body to get rid of harmful substances caused by tobacco smoke. It must be true that when time goes on, the chances of getting a smoking-related problem decrease, but I doubt they are ever eliminated,' replied Lee.

'I'll see if ML1 is ready,' said Cheng, walking to the door. She looked out to the patient area and observed one male patient sat reading a magazine and looked up at Cheng as she spoke, 'ML1.'

'Yes that's me,' he said, getting up. Upon arrival in the treatment room, Lee smiled at ML1.

'Welcome, how are you today?'

'Not too bad. I'm not looking forward to this PH test.'

'Don't worry, it's only one day in a lifetime,' Lee assured the patient. ML1 sat down on the treatment bed and looked at Cheng preparing the kit for him. After checking the kit, Cheng opened the cupboard and took out an anaesthetic spray canister and gave it to Lee who had taken up his position by the patient.

'Right, we will just numb the nose so you don't feel the

discomfort of the tube entering the throat and beyond,' said Lee. ML1 nodded twice and made himself more comfortable on the treatment bed. Five minutes passed and Cheng handed Lee the box and tube. Lee smiled at ML1 and said, 'Okay this is it then. Try to relax and breathe normally.' Lee carefully placed the box on ML1 and attached the clip to his trouser top. Then he inserted the tube carefully into the patient's nostril until it went all the way to the stomach. 'How does that feel?' asked Lee.

'Not too bad,' replied ML1. Lee held up the box and explained the buttons on the front and how they should be used. ML1 stood up and said, 'See you tomorrow then.'

CHAPTER 6

DAY SIX
THE LIBRARY

The morning sunshine poured through the window of the library. GB1 walked over to the window and closed the blind slightly to block the sunlight. She turned around and looked, amazed, at the quantity of books available. There appeared to be more medical books than any other. Also, in one corner of the room there appeared to be every foreign newspaper under the sun. GB1 heard the door open and in walked SG2, who smiled and said, 'Looking for anything in particular?'

'No,' said GB1, 'I'm just a bit bored currently.' SG2 disappeared out of view as GB1 picked up a book and browsed its contents. She quickly placed it back and looked down the shelf for something different.

Meanwhile, at the far corner of the library, SG5 was sitting in a side room reading the Financial Times. He coughed loudly several times. GB1 heard him and took the book she was browsing and entered the side room. 'Good morning, how are you?'

SG5 looked over the top of his glasses and said, 'I'm good and you?'

GB1 sat opposite SG5 and said, 'Yes, alright. How long have you been coughing?'

'About 20 years,' replied SG5.

'I've had it about five years,' said GB1 with a grin. 'Sometimes I get a bit of heartburn too.' SG5 looked serious.

'I get that, but the worse thing is the continuous itchy throat! Every morning without fail I have an unpleasant coughing fit that seems to last a long time.'

'Do you have any food-associated issues?' GB1 asked.

'Don't really know,' said SG5. 'Maybe I will find that out here.'

SG2 arrived at the open door. 'Can I get you two a coffee or tea?'

'I'm fine,' said GB1.

SG5 said, 'I would like a coffee with milk no sugar, thanks.'

'Coming up,' said SG2 and she disappeared. GB1 looked at the book she had taken into the room. SG5 continued reading his newspaper until SG2 arrived with the hot drinks. SG2 placed the tray on the round table, handed one cup to SG5. 'Thank you very much,' said SG5. 'I expect this will make me cough.' He took a sip and a second after had a small coughing fit. 'Told you so,' he remarked.

GB1 looked at SG2 and said, 'Are you still doing some work while you are in here?'

'Yes I am doing some of my accounting duties online,' replied SG2. 'My company is very busy, and we have a lot of month-end reporting. We were due to introduce a new computer system soon, but I have delayed it. It has to be scheduled carefully otherwise there will be a lot of problems to sort out. I mean it's time-consuming anyway, even when things go very well.'

'Where in Singapore do you live?'

SG2 replied, 'I am in Holland Village, in one of the tall tower blocks. It's only an HDB but the location is very good for bars and such.'

GB1 commented, 'Yes I know it quite well. I like the Indian restaurant – The Hot Raj.'

SG2 said, 'Yeah, I have been there a few times myself. My husband likes Indian food.' SG5 took a gulp of coffee and then stood up.

'Must go to the loo, see you in a bit.'

After SG5 had left the room GB1 commented, 'Did we need to know that?' SG2 laughed in agreement.

'So where do you live in Singapore?' SG2 asked.

'I am living in Emerald Hill, just close to Orchard Road,' said GB1.

'Very good,' said SG2.

'Yes, I am very lucky. My husband inherited a nice house from his grandmother. It was a bit of a state and then he was lucky to have the chance to buy the house next door and create two houses in to one.'

'How many bedrooms have you got?' asked SG2.

'We have 12 bedrooms and six bathrooms. Also, four reception rooms, a beautiful conservatory, and a staff flat,' replied GB1.

'Do you have children?' said SG2.

'No just me and my husband. But we often have people staying. We employ two full-time cleaners and a part time gardener.'

SG2 cleared her throat and then drank some coffee. 'How long have you lived in Singapore?'

'I was born here so twenty-nine years,' replied GB1. 'My father handed me his antique business a few years ago. So I am running that with one assistant in Bukit Timah. It's a strange business. Unpredictable. I am importing items from lots of places. I have some nice furniture items from Thailand that should sell well, I think. Also, I managed to obtain a number of Japanese tea sets which are very nice.'

'Sounds interesting,' said SG2.

GB1 stood up, picked up the book, and said, 'I am looking for a book on Chinese Opera. I'm gonna take a look to see if there is anything in this library.' GB1 left the room and a moment later SG5 returned to the room. He sat down and returned to his FT newspaper, folding it carefully so he could read it better.

'I just heard my granddaughter has chicken pox.'

'Oh that's unfortunate,' said SG2.

'She'll be fine, it's just a kid's thing.'

SG2 asked, 'What was your profession?'

SG5 replied, 'I was a second tier Geography teacher. Loved it. My early days were at Yishun Secondary School and then I taught at Pasir Ris Secondary School. It was great fun. But, in the early days, class sizes were large and some of the kids were very poor.'

Meanwhile, in the treatment room, ML1 was lying down on the treatment bed having his catheter removed by Professor Lee. ML1 blinked repeatedly and seconds after the catheter was fully out of his body, he sneezed loudly. 'Sorry about that,' he said.

'Don't worry, just a bit of nose irritation. How do you feel now to be free of the catheter?' asked Lee.

'Yes, it's good to have it gone,' replied ML1.

Lee handed the catheter and box to Nurse Cheng. Cheng disconnected the catheter from the box and then placed a new lead and plugged it in to a computer nearby. ML1 sat up straight and looked at Lee as he spoke. 'Now we'll see how your readings are.' The computer made a whirring noise. Lee pressed buttons on the box and waited. Cheng filled a small glass of water and handed it to ML1.

'Thanks, that's great,' ML1 said, taking the glass and having a large gulp. He then burped softly. The computer made another whirring noise. Lee looked at the screen for a moment.

'Right, it appears that the PH analysis is a normal reading. Total reflux is a little higher than normal but ok. Did you eat and drink as normal in the last 24 hours?'

ML1 replied, 'Yes. I had all my meals at the hospital. Maybe I have eaten less than I would do at home but otherwise okay,' said ML1.

Lee said, 'Okay you're free to go. We will have a bit more info to come out of the computer later, but I think nothing out of normal limits.'

'Okay, thanks,' said ML1 and he left the treatment room quickly.

Five minutes passed and ML2 knocked at the door and entered. Her box was attached to a thick black belt and held lightly by her right hand as she walked to the treatment bed and made herself comfortable. 'How was it?' inquired Lee.

'Alright, well, a little uncomfortable,' said ML2, smiling. Lee removed the equipment from his patient carefully and handed it to Nurse Cheng. Cheng disconnected the catheter and fixed the cable in the box and connected it to the computer. Lee waited for the information to load. After a couple of minutes, he looked at ML2, smiling, and said, 'Looks good. No significant reflux, and acid is low. I presume the box was working okay between red and green lights?'

'Yes,' said ML2.

'I was seeing a green light when I wanted and a red light when turned off.'

'Okay then, you are free to leave,' said Lee. ML2 thanked him and Nurse Cheng and left the room.

CHAPTER 7

DAY SEVEN
ELECTRIC SHOCK TEST

Dr Wong pulled the curtains back to reveal the 'Electric Shock Machine'. It stood all of 14 feet high with a complicated array of wires and leads coming from a box to the side of a comfortable chair. Wong opened the outer door and noticed that the seat still had its plastic wrapping on it. He ripped it off quickly and screwed it up neatly in his hands. He looked at the machine with great interest.

The door to the treatment room opened quickly and Dr Audrey Tan entered. 'Hello Fu,' she said.

'Audrey, what a monster of a machine,' smiled Wong.

'Yes, it's a South Korean-made machine and has some success in sorting ailments like persistent coughs,' added Tan. Wong stood next to the machine and threw the plastic he had been holding into a waste bin. He then stepped inside the machine for further inspection.

'Did you use this monster when you were working in Seoul?' he asked.

'Yes, I did. It was mainly young patients due to the electric volts coming through.'

'Did any patients have bad side effects?' inquired Wong.

'Some patients have had headaches and bad dreams, but nothing serious,' said Tan.

Wong stepped out of the machine and took another

lingering look and then faced Tan. 'Well, we better start the Pre-Test check then.'

Tan replied. 'Yes, SG3 will be due here in about an hour so we need to go through the procedure. I remember it quite well from my Seoul days but have the manual on the desk here.' Tan picked up the manual which had the letters 'EST' engraved in gold at the front. It looked like an encyclopaedia. Tan flicked through several pages and then looked at Wong. 'I remember a Korean lady in her late twenties who had coughed quite badly for around ten years. She had the Electric Shock Test and was completely cured of the cough. The theory in Seoul was that the digestion system received a boost and seemed to reduce the amount of acid in the stomach.'

'Interesting,' commented Wong. 'A lot of body functions could change if receiving an electric current'.

'Pre-Test 1 says check all wires and leads are secure, anything loose needs to be connected to the right area. All wiring is labelled and all connecting points are also labelled with the same number.' Tan cleared her throat and continued. 'Pre-Test 2 says ensure that the EST machine's software is connected to your computer. Ah, I set that up with an engineer three weeks ago and it was fine from what I can remember.'

Wong entered the machine, followed by Tan. They each started checking the wiring was connected properly. Wong said, 'I found a wire with no reference number.' Tan walked over to take a look herself. She looked at both sides of the grey wire and a second look found the number. 'Sometimes the number is in the same colour as the wire, so it is difficult to pick it up,' said Tan. 'Look, you can just see the reference number in grey on grey. It's easy to miss it.'

'Okay I see it,' said Wong. They continued with the inspection until it was complete.

Tan walked to the PC monitor that sat in the middle of a small desk, turned it on, and waited for it to boot up. Wong walked over to the desk and stood behind Tan and looked at the screen.

Various messages appeared then a menu popped up. 'Looks like we're ready to go,' said Tan. 'I'll just see if our patient has arrived outside.' Tan left the treatment room and returned a minute later followed by SG3.

'Good morning, SG3,' Wong welcomed the patient. SG3 nodded without speaking. Tan showed SG3 to the treatment bed a few feet away from the EST machine.

'Wait there a while,' she said and then walked over to her computer and typed in some data. Wong walked to the back of machine and switched on the electric supply. After few seconds there was a whirring sound and then a slight vibration noise.

Tan walked over to SG3 and said, 'Would you like to take the seat in the machine, and I'll get you fixed up?' SG3 took off his gown and handed it to Tan, leaving him in only his underpants. Tan threw the gown on to the chair outside the machine and looked at SG3. 'Are you comfortable?'

'I'm okay,' said SG3. Tan took two wires with yellow tabs and fixed one to each arm. She followed up with two wires with blue tabs at the end and placed one on each thigh.

'Okay, this will be our first test. Just relax. It should be just vibration,' said Tan, reassuringly. SG3 sat motionless and looked very worried. Tan left the machine and closed the door and walked over to the computer. After some typing Tan returned to the front of the machine and stood side by side with Wong. Tan had a remote device in her hand to control the test.

Tan and Wong looked at each other, Tan said, 'Here we go then. Alright, SG3, we will start now.' SG3 nodded without saying anything. Tan pressed a button on the remote and a loud humming noise increased rapidly and then subsided slightly. After three minutes Tan switched it off. Tan sought reassurance from SG3 that he was feeling fine. 'How was the experience?'

'Not too bad,' said SG3. 'I have a slight tingle in both arms but not the legs.' Tan opened the door and entered the machine. She picked up more wires from the floor and fixed them to the chest, back, and head. The patient now had the humiliation of 10 different attachments to his body. Tan left the machine and closed the door. As she walked over to the computer, Wong was looking at it and reading the data.

'First test result unremarkable,' said Wong.

Tan commented, 'I think the machine is monitoring all usual body functions like breathing, heartbeat, and blood pressure.' Wong moved to the side so that Tan could work on the computer. Tan quickly typed for a few minutes and then returned to stand in front of the machine. Wong stayed behind the computer to view the next test. Tan warned SG3 that the second test was about to commence. SG3 smiled and said, 'Bring it on.' Tan looked at the remote device and pressed the start button. This time the hum was louder, and the patient began to twitch and blink repeatedly, and his hands shook slightly from side to side. After three minutes Tan stopped the test and waited for half a minute and then entered the machine. She put her right hand on the patient's shoulder.

'How are you feeling?' she asked.

SG3 looked up from his seat and said, 'A little bit shaken up.'

'Any dizziness?' asked Tan.

'A bit, yes,' replied the patient.

'Okay we will have a ten-minute break and then do the third and final test.'

Ten minutes had passed, and Tan entered the machine again. She took the remaining wiring and attached them to the patient's hands, feet, and stomach. Now SG3 was sitting with sixteen electric current leads attached to his body. Tan exited the machine but left the door open and walked over to the wall cupboards. She opened a cupboard and took out a set of soundproof earmuffs. Tan quickly took them over to SG3 and fitted them securely to his ears and over his head. Tan walked out of the machine and closed the door. She looked at SG3 and raised her hand with her thumb extended to indicate that the test was about to start. Tan paused for a moment, then pressed the button on the remote to start the test. This time the humming was very loud and continued being loud, unlike the previous two tests that had slightly subsided after the opening seconds. SG3 looked worried to death and was visibly moving around in his chair by the actions of the electric currents being fed into his body. Wong looked worried and said to Tan, 'Is he going to be alright?'

'He'll be fine,' Tan replied. 'He'll just be a bit shaken and tired after the final test.' The minutes passed by and SG3 looked troubled. His face went red and sweat began to roll down his face. He turned his head around in a circular motion and at the same time his legs kicked out. Tan said, 'Four minutes gone, just one more and we are finished.' The final minute seemed endless. The patient looked extremely uncomfortable. Tan pressed the remote button to stop the test.

The humming and vibration subsided. SG3 moaned like a sick dog. When the noise had stopped, Tan entered the machine and removed the earmuffs first and then quickly removed all the wiring from SG3. He was motionless, like a zombie. Tan placed both her hands on his shoulders and kept them there for a few minutes. Tan looked down at SG3 just as he was opening his eyes. 'How are you feeling?' she asked. SG3 looked at her, disgusted.

'I am feeling terrible.'

Tan said, 'You better sit quiet for a while and try to relax.' Wong looked on, worried, and then switched his attention to the computer. Tan left the machine and switched off the electric at the back. Tan returned to the front of the machine to view the patient, who was still in considerable discomfort but with eyes open and blinking, trembling slightly. Tan walked over to the computer and started typing. SG3 stood up and wobbled. He then stepped out of the machine and fell over on to the floor as if he had been shot. Wong and Tan quickly went to his aid. SG3 rolled over and laid on his back.

'Am I dead?' he gasped.

Wong wiped the patient's head with a paper towel and said, 'Just try and relax for a moment.' Tan ran to the sink and poured water into a small tumbler. Wong helped SG3 sit up and he took a small sip.

Meanwhile, in a small treatment room, Nurse Cheng was taking the weekly blood pressure checks. In the chair was SG1. Cheng wrapped the device around the patient's arm and pressed the button on the box to start. SG1 looked at the numbers flicking over on the machine. At the finish point Cheng read out the result, '160 over 85, not great.'

'I've often had high blood pressure,' said SG1.

'Do you take any medication for it?' asked Cheng.

'No, perhaps I should,' said SG1. Cheng removed the cloth from his arm.

'Yes, ask your doctor for some medication. We'll see over the coming weeks what an average reading is, okay?' said Cheng.

'I'll do that,' said SG1, adjusting his shirt sleeve and standing up. They exchanged goodbyes.

After a few minutes the next patient arrived in the treatment room. SG2 walked over to the seat next to where the nurse was sitting. Cheng smiled at SG2. 'Just role your sleeve up so I can wrap the cloth round.' SG2 made her upper arm available. Cheng wrapped the cloth around the patient's arm and pushed the button. 'How was your BP the last time you had it checked?' asked Cheng.

'I don't remember any previous problems,' replied SG2. The machine made its whirring noise and then subsided. Cheng looked at the box and waited for the reading.

'121 over 81,' she said. 'That's very good.' SG2 smiled in agreement. Cheng removed the cloth and said, 'Okay, you are free to go.'

'Thanks,' said SG2 and she left the treatment room.

Five minutes passed and SG5 arrived for his BP test. He sat in the chair and immediately fell into a loud coughing fit. 'Oh dear, let me get you some water,' said Cheng. Still coughing, SG5 took the beaker of water from Cheng and drank half in one go.

'That's better,' he gasped.

'Your cough is bad,' said Cheng.

'You can say that again,' said SG5, taking another sip of water.

'If you are okay now, please make your arm available for the BP cloth,' said Cheng. SG5 rolled up his shirt sleeve. Cheng attached the cloth and pressed the button on the box. SG5 picked up his water and drank it. 'Would you like any more?' Cheng asked.

'Half a cup would be great,' replied SG5. Cheng walked to the sink and half filled and then gave it to SG5. 'Thanks a lot,' said SG5. The machine had got to its reading.

Cheng looked and read it out to the patient. '150 over 91, it is a bit high.'

'Probably because I just had a coughing fit,' suggested SG5. Cheng raised her eyebrows.

'Yes maybe, we'll wait five minutes and do another test.'

Cheng got up and went to the worktop and sink area and tidied up various medical items and placed them in the cupboards above. Cheng looked at her watch and waited a moment and then re-joined SG5 and placed the BP cloth on his arm and pressed the button. The patient and nurse both waited in anticipation of the new reading. '139 over 82, better,' said Cheng.

'I'll take that,' said SG5, smiling.

Cheng removed the BP cloth and said, 'Thank you very much, hope you enjoy the rest of the day.'

'Cheers,' said SG5. He straightened his shirt sleeve and got up from his seat. He left the treatment room. Cheng wrote in the patient's file and then closed it shut. Cheng picked up the phone and dialled.

'Professor Lee, Cheng here, I have completed the blood

pressure tests for today.' She listened to the response. 'Oh dear, SG3 alright. Hallucinations, it was a new experiment and carried some risks … Right, see you later.'

CHAPTER 8

DAY EIGHT
WEEK 1 REVIEW

Professor Lee walked quickly to the meeting room and entered. 'Good morning, all,' he said, looking around the room to see if everyone was present. 'Looks like we are all here except for SG3. He's still recovering from the Electric Shock Test he had yesterday!' Lee opened the notebook that he had brought along to the meeting.

Lee looked around the patients and fixed his gaze on SG1. 'Tell us briefly how your first week has gone here?'

'Well, no change so far,' said SG1. 'I had a barium swallow test. It felt strange, drinking in all those different positions. But all seemed to go well. I am coughing with about the same frequency as before taking the new drug.'

Lee nodded approval, 'Okay, how about you, SG2?'

'I spent a bit of time in the library the other day, looking for any medical information on the cough problem but could not see any books on the matter.'

'There should be. Take another look,' said Dr Wong.

'I will do,' said SG2.

The door to the meeting room burst open and there in the doorway was SG3, standing red-faced. 'Sorry I cannot be at the meeting today. I am still feeling the effects of my electric shock test,' he gasped. 'In fact, I have to apologise.' Tears rolled down his face. 'Just now I have had an accident and left a trail of shit down the corridor, diarrhoea shit, I'm so sorry.' Professor Lee stood up and walked out with SG3.

'You need to have complete rest. I'll get some medication sent to your room,' said Lee. SG3 thanked Lee and disappeared down the corridor. Lee returned to the meeting room where Dr Malinowski was on the phone. 'Jenny, unfortunately a patient has made a mess in corridor four outside the meeting room. Can you get it cleaned up straight away? … Thanks.'

Lee sat down again. 'Okay let's resume our weekly review to see how people have been getting on in our first week. SG4, how was your first week?'

'Actually, I have not felt good this week. My cough has been worse than normal, and I've had some problems swallowing food. It feels like there may be an obstruction in the throat.' Dr Wong looked concerned.

'We better take a look tomorrow. Have you any other symptoms?'

SG4 cleared her throat and said, 'Well a bit of stomach pain and other times heartburn. So, yes, I have some current concerns.'

Lee nodded at SG4. 'We'll do some tests tomorrow.' Then he looked at the side of the table where SG5 was sitting. 'SG5, how has it been for you?' said Lee.

SG5 stuttered. 'The only problem I had was difficulty in sleeping. Other than that, my situation is as before I came into the hospital.'

Lee asked, 'Have you any previous experience with sleeping tablets?'

'Not that I can remember,' said SG5.

Lee shuffled some papers and then looked around the

table for ML1. 'ML1, how was your first week then?'

'Basically I have been okay.' Lee looked at his notes.

'You had a barium swallow test and results were ok. Normal acid, a bit of air reflux was found. Er, no fungus, no abnormalities really. You've noticed nothing unusual in the way you feel, day to day?'

'Actually, I had a bit of stomach-ache ten minutes after taking MK888 on three occasions. But it didn't last for long,' replied SG5. Lee looked at his notes again and then looked up towards ML2.

'ML2 how's it going for you?' ML2 looked at Lee and said. 'No side effects and everything feels normal.' Lee looked at his notes.

'You had a barium swallow test which didn't show anything abnormal. Okay how about HK1?'

'Well, I think I have coughed a bit less since taking MK888,' said HK1. Lee and Wong looked at each other and smiled. Wong's grin stayed as he turned to look at HK1.

'Do you mind keeping a daily record to see how much you think the medication is helping?'

'I can do that,' agreed HK1.

Lee added, 'Obviously while under the experiment in this hospital, you are not smoking much and hopefully not drinking outside these four walls at all!'

'Yes, that's right, I am avoiding alcohol and only smoking outside the hospital a few times a day.'

'Good,' said Lee shuffling his notes. 'How's about GB1?'

GB1 cleared her throat. 'I have a slightly reduced cough and heartburn but a couple of times in the morning after taking MK888 I had a minor headache, don't know if there is a connection.'

'Okay, again, keep a record,' said Lee.

Lee looked around the table and nodded at TW1. 'TW1, how is your first week?' TW1 looked nervous and spoke as if worried.

'Well, I am coughing a bit more than normal and it feels like I have a slight blockage in the throat.'

Lee looked a bit concerned. 'You better have an examination tomorrow. Try not to worry, it's usually nothing.' Lee closed his folder. 'That just about wraps things up for today then, unless anyone has any questions.'

Nobody did and the meeting ended.

CHAPTER 9

DAY NINE
CANCER, OH MY GOD

Nurse Cheng entered the endoscopy room where Dr Malinowski and Dr Wong were already present. Wong was looking at the computer and Malinowski was setting up the endoscopy machine for SG4. Cheng walked over to the machine and looked at Malinowski. 'All set?' said Cheng. Malinowski tightened a screw on the tube.

'I think so. Not sure if SG4 is having this done with sedation or the spray,' said Malinowski.

Cheng turned on the computer monitor attached to the endoscopy device and checked the details.

'We are taking a close look at the throat today, to see if there is anything amiss,' called Wong from the back of the room. Malinowski looked to Wong.

'We might do a biopsy if we find anything suspicious.'

'Yes, we'll do that,' replied Wong.

Cheng looked at the monitor and said, 'We are ready for the patient now.'

Cheng walked over to the medicine cupboard and took out a small canister of anaesthetic spray ready for the procedure and took it over to the table next to the endoscopy machine. The telephone rang on the desk where Wong was sitting. He picked it up, 'Hello, Wong here … Okay thanks Jenny.' He placed the phone down. 'SG4 is ready for the test.'

Cheng washed her hands at the sink quickly.

'I'll go and collect her then,' she said, looking at Wong. Cheng dried her hands and walked to the door quickly, she disappeared for a minute and then returned with SG4. SG4 smiled and said, 'Hello' to the two doctors. They smiled back and asked her to sit on the treatment bed. Malinowski picked up a check list on a clip board and sat down next to SG4.

'I am just going to go through a few checks with you and explain the procedure of the gastroscopy which will last five or ten minutes. A little longer if we take any biopsies. Now, can you confirm that you have only administered water in the last twelve hours?'

'Yes, that is correct,' replied SG4.

'This procedure of gastroscopy will involve placing a tube in your mouth, passing through your throat, all the way down to your stomach and intestines. If we see anything unusual, we may take a biopsy. This will not cause you any pain and the total time of the procedure is likely to be between ten to fifteen minutes. Okay so far?'

'Yes, I think so,' said SG4.

Malinowski continued, 'There are some possible risks which are as follows – bleeding from the biopsy or where a polyp has been removed; change to the heart rate; a sore throat; slight bruising to the lining of the oesophagus—'

SG4 coughed twice then said, 'Please continue.'

'A probe will be attached to your finger to monitor the heart rate throughout. For this procedure you can choose to have a minor anaesthetic spray to the throat which will make it numb, or you can choose to be put to sleep by a sedative injection in your hand. The only thing is with this one you will feel worse after the procedure has ended. Which one do you want to choose?'

SG4 thought for a moment and then said, 'As it's only a short while I will go for the throat spray and stay awake.' Malinowski nodded and turned to Cheng.

'Asterina, can you administer the spray to the patient's throat?'

Cheng smiled at SG4 and said, 'Would you like to lay down on the treatment bed and open your mouth as wide as you can?'

Nervously SG4 said, 'Alright.' Cheng moved close to SG4 and put the small canister in her mouth and sprayed hard for five seconds. Cheng smiled at SG4.

'It'll sting and feel itchy. Just relax.' SG4 sneezed and then coughed. 'Are you alright?' asked Cheng.

'Fine,' said SG4, making herself more comfortable on the treatment bed.

'We will let that anaesthetic to do its work on your throat and then we'll start the test in a few minutes.' SG4 nodded. Cheng grabbed the heart monitor and placed it on the patient's finger. 'This is to monitor the heart throughout. I'm also going to put a mouth guard on your teeth so this will protect your teeth and gums.' Cheng attached a top and bottom guard to the patient's teeth.

Wong and Malinowski were looking at the computer on the desk, some distance from SG4 and Cheng. Wong whispered to Malinowski, 'We may find something today.'

Malinowski looked at Wong. 'Yes, that is worrying me too,' she whispered so that SG4 could not here the conversation.

Malinowski walked over to the treatment bed, leaving Wong at the desk. Malinowski smiled at SG4. 'Are we relaxed and ready to go?'

'Let's do it' smiled SG4. Cheng started up the machine and grabbed the endoscopy tube and handed it to Malinowski. Malinowski looked at the end to confirm the light was on.

'Ok, SG4, we will start the test now,' said Malinowski. 'You should not be in too much discomfort but there may be an occasion or two when you gag. This is completely normal and nothing to worry about. If it does become unbearable at any point raise your arm and we will stop the test.' SG4 nodded in agreement. Malinowski placed the tube very slowly in the patient's mouth and looked to the monitor to view the insides of the patient. The tube was pushed further and then stopped. Malinowski stared at the monitor.

'Dr Wong, could you take a look at the screen?' Wong walked quickly to the endoscopy monitor and looked at the screen.

'I don't know,' he remarked. 'Better take a biopsy of both of them,' he concluded. Malinowski clicked the endoscopy and took two biopsies from the area near to the patients' vocal cords. 'That's fine, Aneleise,' said Wong, studying the procedure on the screen.

Malinowski continued the test with the tube being pushed further and further down the oesophagus. Malinowski and Wong watched the screen with intense concentration. SG4 laid still throughout and scratched her leg slightly. Malinowski brought the tube back from the stomach all the way out of the patient and handed the tube to Cheng. Malinowski said, 'Can you release the biopsy box and place it on the counter so I can take it down the laboratory straight away?' Cheng carried out the task quickly.

Wong took the probe off the patient's finger and asked

her to open her mouth so that the teeth guard could be taken out. Malinowski walked to the sink and washed her hands and then picked up biopsy sample box and left the room. Wong adjusted the treatment bed so that SG4 could be more comfortable. 'How are you feeling now?' asked Wong.

'A little dizzy,' said SG4. Cheng handed SG4 a glass of water. 'Thank you,' SG4 said gratefully.

Wong sat facing SG4 'We carried out a thorough endoscopy and did find something we need to check out,' said Wong.

SG4 sat up straight away and said, very concerned, 'What did you find?'

Wong hesitated for a moment and then said, 'There appears to be two lumps on the vocal cords. One was quite large and the other one small. Dr Malinowski has taken a biopsy down to the lab to find out more.'

SG4 coughed loudly and then cried out, 'Oh my god, I've got cancer.'

Wong tried to reassure the patient. 'You should not jump to conclusions without the medical evidence. We will have the lab tests tomorrow.' SG4 started sweating badly and looked very worried. Cheng handed her a towel which SG4 gratefully accepted.

CHAPTER 10

DAY TEN
IN THE LABORATORY

Dr Malinowski sat in the laboratory looking down through a microscope. The telephone rang next to her. Malinowski picked up the phone 'Malinowski, uh yes, I have studied the reports on Xenoxaphide but not Polydixophine and Chenishdoroxide … Well, Xenoxaphide is interesting. The trials have been quite successful so far. As with regards to side effects, some patients suffered mild headaches and some patients were seen to have a rash on their arm … The sample was 500 in three European countries … Okay I'll let you know about Polydixophine and Chenishdoroxide. I have been busy lately and we have this big MK888 testing going on at the moment … Well it's early days but we gave one patient the Electric Shock Treatment and he suffered quite badly … It was a Singapore national, male, twenty years old. Yeah, I think he's had many dizzy spells and diarrhoea … It was only three days ago. He'll be alright I'm sure … Okay speak to you again soon.'

Malinowski made herself a coffee and then returned to her microscope. She removed one slide and put a new slide in for examination. After a lingering study, Malinowski had a rest and stared into space. She then looked again for a few minutes, adjusting the microscope to analyse the slide. Malinowski spoke softly to herself and released herself from the machine. 'Cancer, oh my god.' After a moment motionless, she picked up the phone called Dr Wong. 'Fu, Aneleise here. Can you pop in to the lab? I have some results for SG4.' Two minutes passed, and Wong walked through the door briskly.

'What have you got then?' he questioned.

'The two growth biopsies from SG4 are malignant. I think stage two throat cancer,' said Malinowski.

Wong shook his head, 'That's not good.' Malinowski picked up the patient's notes folder and looked at various pages and then stopped.

'SG4 has had haemoptysis on two occasions in the last year,' said Malinowski.

'We will ask her if she can link that to anything else,' remarked Wong.

Malinowski continued 'The cough's history is some four years. The patient is an ex-smoker, no specific number of cigarettes per day. What's your view on the time it takes for an ex-smoker to rid themselves of any dangerous substances?'

Wong replied, 'Now you got me on that one. This is one of the unresolved and unclear medical theories that divides opinions. I don't know. But I would say after ten years it gets less and less likely that previous smoking can come out somewhere. You see, everyone is different in their physical ability to deal with bad things in the body. Also, I think if you look at an ex-smoker who had a generally active lifestyle with no other bad habits versus an ex-smoker who also drinks a lot of alcohol and took no exercise then the later life scenarios will be different.'

'Yeah, I think I agree with your view,' said Malinowski, shaking her head.

There was a soft knock at the door. 'Come in,' said Malinowski. SG4 entered with a worried look on her face.

'Can we talk?' she said.

'Sure,' said Wong, pointing to the chair near the desk.

'How has it been the last twenty-four hours?' asked Malinowski.

'Not good,' moaned SG4. 'I have not slept very well and I haven't eaten much due to worrying about my condition.'

'That's understandable,' said Wong. Wong and Malinowski pulled up chairs so they could sit very close to SG4. Wong looked at SG4 with a serious expression.

'Dr Malinowski analysed the biopsy we took from your throat and found evidence of stage two cancer. While this is obviously bad news, it may have not spread to other organs. You will need to contact your main doctor straight away in order to see a cancer specialist, ASAP.' SG4 cried out loud. Wong grabbed a tissue and handed it to SG4. She took it gently and blew her nose and wiped her eyes. SG4 coughed slightly and continued.

'I have to face whatever treatment is coming to me. It's not good but I pray I can get through it.' Wong looked at Malinowski and then back to SG4.

'We cannot tell you what your treatment will be. Every cancer patient has an individual treatment course. Dr Malinowski and I are not experts on cancer-related patients.' SG4 looked at Wong and then turned down to the ground. Wong continued, 'I suggest you take a few days away from this hospital, see your doctor and decide if you want to continue with this experiment or not. Any cancer treatment you eventually get is unlikely to be for a number of weeks so you will be able to complete the experiment if you want to. I don't want to put you under any pressure to complete this MK888 test. It's up to you and your doctor and cancer specialists to say if it's okay or not.'

SG4 coughed twice, 'I'll do as you suggest, get an appointment with my doctor to organise a meeting with a cancer specialist. Then, I'll get back to you later about continuing the MK888 test.'

'Okay then,' said Wong.

Malinowski added, 'Try not to worry. I know it's hard, but you will get through it I'm sure. A positive outlook does help and the cure rate is getting better every year.' SG4 stood up.

'Thank you for the information and I'll be in touch when I know my movements.'

'Good luck,' Wong and Malinowski said simultaneously. SG4 left the laboratory.

Wong looked at Malinowski and said, 'I just hope she does not have to go through radiotherapy. I had an old school friend who underwent eight weeks of it and the side effects were terrible.'

Malinowski frowned, looking at the closed door through which her stricken patient had just walked.

CHAPTER 11

DAY ELEVEN
LOSING MONEY

HK1 was sitting in his room watching TV. A horse race meeting from Sha Tin, Hong Kong. The small TV was on a suspended arm from the wall. HK1 studied the runners in his newspaper on his lap. He drank half a cup of water and sighed heavily. The race started with commentary. 'And they're off for this 1,600 metre Dragongate restaurant handicap. Number Eight takes a one length lead over Kong Bong Song followed by Royal Moment. As they continue on, King's Table is struggling at the rear. They have covered two hundred metres and it's still Number Eight continuing to lead with Kong Bong Song in close pursuit. Slowly Before is making headway and King's Table is now some way behind in the rear.' HK1 looked at the TV intensely and started shouting.

'Come on, Mr Big Prawn.'

The commentary on the race continued, 'Number Eight is weakening now at the halfway stage and the new leader is Slowly Before. Slowly Before is in the lead by one, followed by King Bong Song still travelling well. Then a further one back is After Thought. Mr Big Prawn is making headway and only four lengths behind with around two hundred metres to go.'

'Come on, Mr Big Prawn, come on, Mr Big Prawn!'

The commentary continued, 'Slowly Before is being joined

by Kong Bong Song and Mr Big Prawn taking third place. As they fly past the 100 metre point it is Kong Bong Song in the lead followed by Mr Big Prawn as Slowly Before fades ...' HK1 belted his newspaper up and down on his bed as the race came to its conclusion, shouting encouragements to Mr Big Prawn. The race concluded; 'King Bong Song holds on a head to beat Mr Big Prawn and Slowly Before finishes third.'

HK1 shook his head from side to side and screamed 'Second again, I don't believe it.'

HK1 leapt on his bed and picked up The Straits Times and looked for the race details of the evening's race meeting at The Turf Club in Singapore. He read the paper for five minutes and then dozed off. After three hours HK1 awoke and grabbed the clock on the table. It was five o' clock in the afternoon. The TV was still on and a game show was under way. HK1 grabbed the remote control and turned the TV off. Sitting up in the bed he grabbed the phone and dialled. 'Could I have a taxi from ENT Hospital, Cairnhill Circle, to the Turf Club in Kranji .... about six p.m. ... Oh, how far is it? ... 21 km, and how long will it take? .... Around thirty minutes, that's great, thanks.' HK1 put the phone down and went to the bathroom for a shower.

Fresh from the shower HK1 dressed quickly in light clothing as the night at the races would be very warm. After dressing he picked up The Straits Times newspaper and neatly tore off the racing pages to take with him for the evening. He studied the pages very closely for around half an hour till the phone rang and the receptionist informed him that the taxi had arrived to take him to the racecourse. Grabbing his wallet and a pen, he placed them in his shirt pocket and left the room speedily. Jumping into the taxi outside the hospital he exchanged hellos with the driver.

The driver said, 'Anything picked out for tonight's card?' HK1 removed the carefully folded newspaper from his pocket and read out to the taxi driver.

'I like the chance of East Coast Runner in the eight o' clock race. He was third in his first race of the season and will be fully fit now. Plus, an extra two hundred metres should suit very well.'

'Interesting,' remarked the driver. He continued 'I had a tip for Mr Moonlight in the seven o' clock. The horse has no form at all. What are the predicted odds in your paper?' HK1 studied the details of the seven o' clock race.

'The prediction is twenty to one, the horse has had eleven races in its career and never better than fourth place. I'll invest a bit on it, thanks.' The car came to abrupt stop. A pedestrian has crossed the road just as the lights changed. The driver wound down the window.

'You should be more careful,' he screamed at the guy he had almost run over.

The man shouted back 'You drive too fast.' The driver continued with the journey, shaking his head.

'Some of these people are idiots. Taking silly chances.' HK1 nodded in agreement.

The early evening traffic in Singapore was heavy and the journey to the racecourse took fifty minutes where it might have been half that at another time of the day. HK1 paid the driver and walked to the entrance of The Turf Club with an exciting state of mind. There were people everywhere. It was extremely busy. HK1 chose the middle-priced enclosure for his evening entertainment. He walked to a bar and ordered a large whiskey. When it arrived, he added the same amount of water and then drank it all in one go. He then immediately started coughing for a few seconds.

He cleared his throat and took the newspaper cutting from his pocket and looked at the race runners. Two races went by before the first bet was struck. The taxi driver had given HK1 a tip for Mr Moonlight in the seven o' clock race. The odds on the tote were twenty to one. HK1 smiled to himself and thought he better go and look at the horse in the pre-parade paddock. To check on his wellbeing. HK1 walked down the steps to the paddock and looked at all the horses parading. After about ten horses had walked by, Mr Moonlight appeared. The horse walked confidentially and its coat was shining with little diamond imprints. HK1 thought the horse was worth a bet. Turning away from the paddock, HK1 headed for the tote window and waited his turn in the que for people placing bets.

'A hundred dollars, win, number two,' he said firmly. The odds had changed. It appeared the horse was heavily backed. HK1 looked at his tote voucher which stated, should the horse win, he would collect one thousand seven hundred dollars. Effectively a horse at sixteen to one. HK1 made sure he had a good view in the grandstand. The race started around half a minute late due to one horse not wanting to enter the stalls. Mr Moonlight was slow out of the stalls but quickly made up ground to take fourth place around the first bend. Gradually, as the race unfolded, Mr Moonlight got to the front a hundred metres from the finish and held on to win by half a length. HK1 clapped his hands in excitement. The taxi driver had put sixteen hundred dollars in his pocket. A nice start to the evening.

The next race went by without a bet. Then it was time for

the eight o' clock race. The race that HK1 had come for. East Coast Parkway was the selection and after checking out the horses' wellbeing in the paddock, HK1 decided to place a bet. Nervously arriving at the tote window, he told the lady, 'Two thousand dollars, win, number seven.' His trembling fingers pushed the bundle of dollars notes over. He looked at the tote ticket, win dividend would be four thousand dollars. The odds for East Coast Parkway were only evens. HK1 was a bit disappointed as had hoped for a better return. The race started five minutes late due to several runners refusing to enter the stalls at the first attempt. East Coast Parkway was quickly out of the stalls and took a lead. At the halfway stage the horse had a four-length lead and was looking good for a win. But as they got close to the winning post, Red Hot Chilli, the second favourite, snatched the race from East Coast Parkway to win a short head. HK1 was devastated. His throat was sore from shouting the horse's name. He slumped to the ground and held his head in his hands. 'Shit fuck, shit fuck,' he cried out loud.

HK1 made his way to the toilet and then entered a cafeteria restaurant and selected a chicken dish, a prawn dish, and egg fried rice. A Chinese tea completed his order. He carried his meal to a table that was empty apart from two elderly men discussing the next race. HK1 ate his meal quickly and left the restaurant. He noticed an upmarket-looking bar and entered it, he walked over to order a drink. 'A treble whiskey,' stormed HK1.

The barman poured the whiskey into a glass then inquired, 'Having a bad night?'

'Sort of,' snapped HK1. 'Still time to make a profit.' HK1 took the newspaper out of his pocket and studied the eight-thirty race. The selection was August Moon Festival. He counted the money from his pocket, it totalled three thousand one hundred. He made two piles, two thousand in one pile and one thousand in the other. He folded each pile of notes in half and returned them to his pocket. Coughing loudly, he got to his feet and had a quick look in the pre-race paddock to see if August Moon Festival was in good shape. The horse was sweating slightly, but it was a sticky night, quite humid.

HK1 decided to invest and made his way to the tote again. Standing in the queue of punters he got one of the two piles of money out of his pocket and counted it quickly. When his turn came, he told the tote lady, 'Two thousand dollars, win, number eleven.' The tote lady rolled her eyes in amazement at the size of the bet, handing over the ticket.

'There you go, two thousand, win, number eleven, good luck sir.'

'Thanks,' said HK1, taking the betting slip and putting it his pocket.

The race started on time and August Moon Festival was close up throughout the race but in the closing stages got blocked in and got to the outside too late and finished third. Beaten about two lengths. HK1 ran to the bar and quickly downed two treble whiskies. Feeling dizzy and sick, he decided not to stay at the racecourse any longer. Staggering outside into the street, he slumped down on a public seat and nodded off to sleep. At about one a.m. HK1 woke up feeling terrible and looked at his watch. He stood up slowly and looked in both directions to see if there were any taxis around. There was very little traffic on the roads and no taxis. Wiping the sweat from his brow he suddenly felt nauseas.

Slumping down to the public seat again he turned to the side and spewed on to the ground by his side. Three, four times he brought up all the whiskies and food he had consumed at the racecourse. After vomiting, he felt faint and sat back on the seat. He closed his eyes and coughed three times. After a few minutes his eyes opened, and the small amount of traffic was a slight blur. He noticed a shop in the distance and staggered over to buy some water. Emerging from the shop he took a swig of water and then noticed a taxi coming towards him. Holding up his hand the taxi stopped. HK1 told the driver to take him back to the ENT Hospital. Upon return to his hospital room, HK1 undressed quickly and got into bed. He began feeling ill again so got out of bed ad and rushed to the bathroom where he had another bout of vomiting.

CHAPTER 12

DAY TWELVE
EAR TESTING

Dr Wong walked into his office to the sound of the phone ringing. He grabbed the phone just in time. 'Wong here … That's good, we were hoping you could complete the course. So, we'll see you tomorrow. Oh, before you go just to let you know we are all going to Jurong Bird Park tomorrow afternoon. I you want to join us. Be at the hospital by 1.30 … See you then, take care.' Wong put the phone down and immediately picked it up again and phoned Professor Lee. 'Professor Lee, Wong here. I just spoke to SG4 and she has decided to complete the MK888 testing. So that's good news … She has an appointment at Singapore General Hospital regarding the throat cancer next week … Yes that's it … See you later in the day, we are doing Ear Testing today … are you familiar with the procedure? … Okay, do you want to pop over for a few minutes? … Great, okay, bye.'

Wong put the phone down and walked to his filing cabinet. After a minute of looking, he found the Ear Test information file. He walked over to the photocopier to make copies of the file. He then placed them on the opposite side of his desk just as Professor Lee walked in. 'Would you like a coffee?' Wong asked.

'I'm okay,' replied Lee. He picked up the photocopies on the desk and started to read. Wong looked at his notes. 'Okay so we are doing basic ear testing using a tuning fork, like this.' Opening a drawer, Wong showed Lee the gadget. Lee nodded. 'Now there is a Weber's Test and a Rinne's Test. The Weber's Test is where you place the vibrating fork in the middle of the forehead and ask the patient if they can hear the fork vibrating and if the sound appears equal from both ears or not. If the patient has normal hearing the sound will be heard centrally. If the patient has hearing loss, and the sound is louder in the weaker ear, this will suggest that there is a conductive hearing loss. If the sound is louder in the better ear, it is more likely to be a sensorineural loss.'

'Can you please explain further?' asked Lee.

Wong replied, 'A conductive hearing loss is when there is a problem transferring sound waves anywhere along the path through the outer ear or middle ear. The sensorineural loss is concerning the inner ear and can be permanent.'

Lee asked, 'Which is more common?'

'There are more cases of sensorineural loss than conductive loss.'

'Right, what about the Rinne's Test?' asked Lee.

'To do a Rinne's Test you strike the tuning fork and hold it vertically with its nearest prong about one centimetre away from the patient's outer ear opening, making sure it is not touching any hair. Then, immediately transfer the fork to the other ear and hold the base at the skull firmly for a few seconds. You then ask the patient which of the two positions was the louder. Normally the patient should hear the first position louder than the second. This is a positive test. If the second is louder, then the test is negative.'

Lee nodded. 'How about a Free Field Voice Test?'

Wong replied. 'Yes, we will do that by whispering from

forty centimetres and from twenty centimetres.'

Lee stood up and smiled. 'That's fine, so we are going to do some of the tests each?'

Wong replied 'Yes if I do five and you do four. We are missing SG4 so, when she returns, we'll find time later in the experiment.' Lee left the room speedily. Dr Wong spent the next two hours seeing patients that had recovered from minor operations recently.

Dr Audrey Tan entered the treatment room and turned on all the lights. She made her way to the instrument cupboard and removed a box of special tuning forks. She tested two by pressing them hard on the worktop. Nurse Asterina Cheng entered.

'Hi Audrey,' she smiled.

'Hi Asterina, how are you?' replied Tan. Cheng walked towards the computer.

'I'm fine, just been in the Theatre this morning. It was a nose operation to remove some polyps.'

'Did it go okay?'

Cheng smiled. 'Yes, everything was fine'.

Cheng looked at her watch and said, 'I think it's time for the first ear test, I'll see if SG1 is in the waiting area.' Tan nodded as Cheng left the room. SG1 was reading a magazine in the waiting area. 'SG1,' Cheng shouted loudly. SG1 rose to his feet quickly. Entering the treatment room, SG1 was beckoned to the patient's chair by Tan.

'How is it going?' she asked.

'I am fine,' SG1 replied. Tan looked briefly at her notes while Cheng sat at the desk looking at the computer. Tan looked at SG1 and smiled. 'Right today we are going to do some ear tests. Have you any previous problems at all with your hearing?'

'No, I have not,' said SG1.

Tan continued, 'Any wax or discomfort from chlorine after swimming?'

SG1 thought for a moment and said, 'I don't remember any problems, I did swim in my younger days but didn't get any earache or discomfort.' The door to the meeting room suddenly opened and Dr Wong burst through.

'Hi everybody,' he smiled. 'Sorry I'm a bit late.' Tan handed the file notes to Wong.

'I have to see a patient in half an hour, so I'll shoot off now, if that's okay?'

'Yes please do,' said Wong, reading the patient's file. Wong put the folder down and faced the patient. Tan left the treatment room and Cheng picked up the tiny fork and held it up in front of SG1. 'We are going to test your hearing with this fork,' he smiled. 'I will hit the fork to make it vibrate and then hold it in the middle of your forehead. Try to concentrate and then tell me if the sound seems the same from both ears or if one ear is hearing better than the other.'

SG1 coughed. 'I have a coughing fit coming on, just bear with me a moment.' SG1 coughed loudly, stopped, and then had another bout of coughing. Cheng quickly got him a beaker of water, which he took gratefully. SG1 drank half the water and swallowed hard. He took a second drink and put the beaker down. 'I am okay to continue now,' he blushed. Wong placed the fork in a box, pressed a button for a few seconds, and then took it out quickly, holding it close to the patient's forehead. SG1 stared at the fork until it stopped vibrating.

Wong put the fork down, asking, 'Did you hear it and was it equal from both ears?'

'I heard it clearly,' said SG1. 'And it was about the same quality from both ears.'

'That's satisfactory then,' said Wong. Cheng made notes for the patient's file.

Wong placed the fork back in the special box and said, 'For the second test I am going to hold the fork close to your ear and at the same time pinch the bottom of your skull on the other side.'

'Right,' said SG1 with a little apprehension. Wong pressed the switch on the box and then released it after a couple of seconds. He quickly placed it close to the ear of SG1 and with his other hand pinched the back of his skull for a while until the fork stopped throbbing. 'Now for the other ear,' said Wong. Wong quickly repeated the procedure for the other ear. Putting the fork down, Wong asked, 'So how was that?'

'Both ears heard it at the same loudness,' said SG1.

'That's fine then,' said Wong. Wong pulled open a drawer and took out an otoscope. He looked at SG1 and smiled. 'Now I will just have a quick look at the inside of each ear. This time it will be more comfortable if you lay on the bed rather than sit up.' SG1 got up from the chair and made himself comfortable on the bed close by. Wong asked, 'Just lay on one side for me.' SG1 did as asked. Wong placed the otoscope device at the edge of the patient's ear and carried out the inspection. After a few minutes he took the device out and prompted the patient to turn over so he could inspect the other ear. The other ear inspection found no problems and Wong smiled at SG1. 'You can sit up now. All okay I think.'

'Thanks,' said SG1 somewhat relieved.

The next patient, SG2, arrived and had a sneezing fit followed by a coughing fit. Wong remarked, 'Not having a good day, hey?' SG2 blew her nose and looked at Wong, smiling.

'Sorry, something has irritated my inner system, I think.' Wong pointed her to the patient's seat. SG2 put her handbag on the floor and folded her arms.

'Relax, there is no discomfort with the tests. Right, we will carry out a few tests involving a vibrating fork, a whisper test, and I have an instrument called an otoscope which will allow me to inspect your inner ears. Have you had any hearing problems or anything else connected to the ear?'

'Not really,' said SG2. 'A slight itchy sensation in the right ear recently.' Wong took the tuning fork and placed it in the box to get the vibrating going. Taking out the fork, he held it in front of his patient and asked her for the sound result. 'The same from both ears,' said SG2.

'That was the Weber's Test. Now I will carry out Rinnie's Test, where I will take the vibrating fork from one ear to the other ear quickly while nipping the bottom of your skull.' SG2 raised her eyebrows.

'Don't worry, it's nothing to worry about,' assured Wong. After the same result Wong then informed the patient, 'I will now whisper from thirty centimetres and forty centimetres to see if you can hear me.' Wong positioned himself thirty centimetres from the patient and whispered, 'Somewhere in Singapore on a Sunday evening. Did you grasp that?'

SG2 smiled and said, 'In Singapore on a Sunday evening.'

'One word was missed – "somewhere",' commented Wong. 'Now I will whisper from forty centimetres.' Wong positioned himself and then said, 'Here we go. Somewhere in Singapore on a Sunday evening.' Wong cleared his throat. 'Did you get that?'

SG2 scratched her face. 'In Singapore on a Sunday evening.'

'Okay, again, just the first word missed. My final test is to look inside your ears with this gadget called the otoscope. Could you just lay on the treatment bed and on one side? This is so I can look at each ear.' SG2 walked over to the bed and laid down on her right side. Wong picked up the otoscope and held it to the ear. 'Just try and lay still,' he told the patient. He placed the gadget slowly just inside the ear. After a minute he took it out. 'Well that ear's fine. If you turn over and lay on your other side for me, please.' SG2 turned over and Wong moved closer to carry out the right ear inspection. After a short while he pulled the otoscope out and then took a second look. Wong placed the otoscope down and looked at SG2. 'Okay, you can go back to the chair now. It seems you have a small amount of wax in the right ear. I will now use the spray gun to get rid of it.' Nurse Cheng took a large bib from the drawer by the worktop, she took it over and placed it on SG2.

'Thanks,' said SG2. Cheng returned to the worktop area and took a spray gun from the drawer and filled it to the top with water. She carried it over to Wong.

'There you go, Doctor, all set.'

'Thanks Nurse Cheng,' said Wong taking the large spray gun from her.

SG2 remarked, 'It's quite large.'

Wong replied, 'Yes, well, it has a lot of water in there. This is a messy procedure but it's only water. You will get a slight tingling sensation, but it won't hurt. The wax you have is not very thick.'

'Okay I'm ready,' laughed SG2. Wong held a cone in one

hand close to the patient's ear and held the spray gun with the other hand, he pulled the trigger. Water splashed over Wong and the floor. He rested for a few seconds then carried out the procedure another two times.

'How does that feel?' he asked.

'It sounds like you're talking louder,' squealed SG2.

'That's a benefit then,' concluded Wong.

Sometime after SG2's tests had concluded and she had returned to her day, Tan returned to the treatment room, ready for the next patient. The patient – SG3 – arrived with a miserable face. His multi-coloured hair was all over the place and looking unkept. Tan, Wong, and Cheng stood together some way from SG3 as he sat on the treatment bed. The medics whispered so SG3 could not hear. SG3 looked at them disrespectfully.

'Could we get on,' he snapped. Tan walked over to SG3, leaving Wong and Cheng at the back of the room, looking on.

Tan looked at SG3 and asked, 'How are you feeling?'

'Not great. Since I went on the Electric Shock Machine, I have not felt normal,' SG3 snapped. Tan tried to look sympathetic.

'The situation should get back to normal soon. There is no known permanent damage from the treatment.'

SG3 didn't look convinced. 'Let's hope so.'

Tan smiled at the patient. 'Right then, so today we are doing a few ear tests, just to see if hearing is normal. This involves a vibrating fork and an otoscope.' SG3 nodded his head slightly but still looked miserable. Tan looked over her shoulder and called to Nurse Cheng, 'Could I have the tuning fork and charge box?' Cheng picked up the two items from the worktop and quickly took them to Tan. 'Thank you,' said

Tan, taking one item in each hand. 'Right, in the first test I will hold a vibrating fork in front of your nose and in the second test I will hold it close to each ear in turn.'

'Alright then,' said SG3. Tan placed the fork into the charge box and waited a few moments to the sound of a gentle hum. 'Here we go,' said Tan, placing the throbbing fork close to the patient's nose for around 10 seconds. 'How's that?' Tan asked.

'It seemed the same from both my ears,' replied SG3. Tan put the fork in the box again and pulled it out, throbbing. She placed the fork near the patient's left ear while pinching the lower left-hand side of the skull. After a few seconds she moved the fork to the other ear and nipped the lower right-hand side of the skull. After a few seconds she took the fork away and placed it on the table. 'So how was the sound, right versus left?'

SG3 said, 'No problem. The sound seemed pretty much the same from both ears.'

'Good,' smiled Tan. 'Right then, we'll do our third and final test. I will whisper to you one sentence from thirty centimetres and another forty centimetres distance.'

'Do it,' snapped SG3.

Tan sat at the required distance and spoke softly, 'Whisper test Singapore five four three two one.' SG3 scratched his head then gave his answer.

'Whisper test Singapore five for three two one.'

'That's exactly right' said Tan, holding her hands together, delighted. 'Okay you can go, thanks for taking part.'

The next patient was SG5, the retired teacher. He arrived ten minutes late. 'Sorry, sorry,' he gasped, rushing to the patient's chair.

Wong sat next to the patient and asked, 'Any history of ear problems with yourself or your family?'

'Not for me,' replied SG5. 'But my father has the ringing in the ears.'

Wong nodded. 'Tinnitus is not good. There is no cure. How old was your father when he got it?'

SG5 scratched his head, 'Uh I think seventy-seven.' Wong looked at the box and placed the tuning fork in it, ready. Wong quizzed his patient again, 'Does your father have it in both ears and is it continuous or does the ringing come and go?'

SG5 thought for a moment. 'It's in both ears and it comes and goes. I think mostly in the early morning and late at night.'

'That's interesting. Well, hopefully you never suffer with it like your father. Right then, we'll do the hearing tests with a fork. I will ask you if you can hear clearly and if it's roughly the same loudness from each ear. Then I will do a whisper test. Oh, I nearly forgot, I will look inside each ear with an otoscope.' Wong turned on the charging box to get the tuning fork throbbing. The green light came on to indicate it was ready. Wong grabbed the fork and held it just in front of the patient's nose. It vibrated for about twenty seconds then subsided and stopped. 'How was it?' asked Wong.

'Yes, quite clear and the same loudness from each ear.'

Wong said, 'Good, now I will use the fork again and hold it close to the ear and then the other ear. While the fork is vibrating, I will nip the bottom of the skull. You alright with that?'

'Yes fine,' said SG5. Wong put the tuning fork back in the box to charge up. Taking the fork out, Wong held it close to the patient's left ear while squeezing the bottom of the skull for ten seconds, then he quickly repeated the process on the other ear. 'Right, what do you think?'

SG5 answered, 'Uh it seemed the same for both ears but, could I ask, er does the tuning fork vibrate a bit less for the second ear?'

Wong shook his head. 'No, the fork has a special motor to keep it vibrating for around twenty seconds at the same speed and then stops quite quickly. We'll do the whisper test next.' Wong got himself in position and whispered, 'A rainstorm in Orchard Road tomorrow.'

SG5 smiled. 'A rainstorm in Orchard Road tomorrow.'

Wong nodded. 'Good. Now I'll speak again from forty centimetres. A rainstorm in Orchard Road tomorrow.'

SG5 looked serious this time. 'I only heard rainstorm in Orchard.'

'Alright, I'll now do the otoscope inspection where I look into the ears for anything amiss. Nurse Cheng, could you bring me the otoscope?' Cheng speedily delivered the otoscope to Wong. Wong thanked her. 'For this test can you lay on your side so I can better position the otoscope?' SG5 immediately laid on his side. Wong positioned himself and quickly inspected both ears. 'They seem normal.'

SG5 sat up and said, 'Thanks doctor.' Wong smiled at SG5. 'You are free to go now, thanks for your time today.'

'Bye,' said SG5, leaving the room.

Wong looked at Tan at the other end of the room. 'I need to do something; can you do the testing for ML1?'

'Okay, no problem.'

'Thanks, Professor Lee will do the last four patients.' Wong left the room and observed ML1 in the waiting room. 'ML1, would you like to go in for your ear test?' ML1 got to his feet quickly and followed Wong to the door of the treatment room where Wong opened the door for the patient and then walked away. ML1 tests revealed a little wax in both ears which was washed out by Dr Tan. The patient left the treatment room with a slight ear-ache after the procedure.

Later, Professor Lee arrived in the treatment room somewhat flustered. Wong had also returned from his errands

'Hello everyone.'

'Hello,' came the response from Tan, Wong, and Cheng. Lee turned to Wong and asked, 'So how were the ear tests so far?'

Wong replied, 'No real problems, just a bit of wax with some patients that we were able to dispose of. Right we'll leave you to it then. Audrey and I have to go to a Medical Council Meeting.'

'Okay have fun.'

Lee looked over to Cheng and asked, 'Who's the next patient for ear testing?' Cheng picked up a brown folder from the desk where she was sitting and handed it to Lee. He opened it. 'Ah our young Malaysian lady.'

Cheng looked at her watch, 'She's due about now so I'll see if she's in the waiting area.' Cheng left the treatment room and returned a few moments later with the patient.

'Come in and take a seat over there,' Lee instructed.

'Thank you,' said ML2.

'Any problems with your ears past or present?' Lee asked.

'No, I do not recall any issues,' replied the patient. Lee took the fork and charge box and sat near to ML2. 'We will do a few simple tests today, starting with this tuning fork that will vibrate rapidly for a short period.'

'Interesting,' remarked ML2, looking at the fork. Lee

charged the fork and smiled at ML2.

'I'll hold the fork in front of your nose and just ask you to concentrate on the sound, is it clear and does the loudness feel the same from both the left and right ears. Is that okay?'

'Fine,' nodded ML2. Lee held the fork in front of the patient until the noise subsided. 'How did it seem?'

'Yes, I think maybe ever so slightly louder in my left ear.'

'Okay, that's fine,' confirmed Lee. 'For the next test I will hold the tuning fork close to your left ear while pinching your lower skull and then quickly change sides to test the other ear.' ML2 nodded her head and appeared a little surprised. Lee carried out the test and the patient said that the sound was clear in both ears. Lee turned around to face Cheng who was sitting at the corner of the room typing on a computer 'Nurse Cheng, could I have the otoscope please?' Cheng sprayed the otoscope with cleaner and dried it with a paper towel and then handed it to Lee. Lee then turned to ML2 and asked the patient to lay on one side so that it was comfortable for the otoscope inspection. Both ears were found to be free of problems. ML2 departed from the treatment room with a smile.

The next patient, HK1, arrived a bit groggy and smelling of alcohol. Lee picked up on the fact and asked the patient if he had been drinking alcohol. 'To be honest I have had one or two drinks.'

'More like three or four,' Lee said angrily. 'We did ask all patients on this experiment to refrain from alcohol and tobacco.' HK1 shrugged his shoulders as if he didn't care. Lee sat next to the patient and held the tuning fork up to HK1. 'Right, this is a tuning fork and I will use it to see if you can hear equally from both ears.' HK1 gazed at the fork and spoke with slurred speech.

'Er how long will it be vibrating for?'

Lee answered, 'Around twenty seconds.'

HK1 rolled his eyes and said, 'Okay let's go.' Lee set up the tuning fork and held it in front of the patient's nose until such time as the vibration stopped. 'How did it sound?' asked Lee.

'Well, it was distinct from the left ear but not from the right ear.' Lee nodded.

'I will be looking at both ears closely in a moment with the otoscope. Before that I will do another test with the tuning fork, where I will hold it close to your ear while pinching the lower part of the skull, and then quickly doing the same to the other ear.'

'Bring it on,' stuttered HK1. Lee prepared the fork again and removed it from the charger and held it against the left ear of the patient and then quickly changed to the right ear for ten seconds. Lee placed the fork on the table beside him. 'Now, HK1, what was the verdict?'

HK1 glared at Lee. 'The sound was there from the left ear but my right ear did not pick up the sound.'

I see,' said Lee, looking a little concerned. 'We'll note in on your file and may have you back for additional testing. I have another thing to do. I will use an otoscope to look closely at each ear. If you could just lay down on your side, it will make it easier for me.'

'No problem,' said HK1, turning over on his left side on the treatment bed. Lee grabbed the otoscope and proceeded to inspect the patient's left ear. 'Just try and lay still, please,' Lee asked. After a while Lee moved the otoscope from the inner ear. 'Well, the left looks normal, let's see if the right ear is ok too, so if you wouldn't mind turning over so I can take a look at the right ear.' Lee inspected the right ear, he took a pause and then looked for a second time. 'I can see a bit of coloured discharge in there. I will get the dispensary to supply you with some ear drops which should help. If it's not better in a week we will have to think of scanning. Ok you are free to go.' HK1 got to his feet quickly and thanked Lee for his time and left the treatment room.

The next patient for ear testing was GB1 who arrived fifteen minutes late. 'Sorry, sorry,' she gasped, making her way to the patient's chair. 'I had an afternoon sleep and lost track of the time.' Lee looked at the woman annoyed but made no comment on her lateness. He walked over to the seat near the patient.

'Have you any ear problems currently or previously?'

'No, none at all,' smiled GB1. Lee picked up the tuning fork and held in it front of his patient. 'This is a tuning fork which I will make throb and there will be a humming noise. The fork will be placed just in front of your nose. It will vibrate for about 20 seconds and then stop. I will then ask you if you heard the humming clearly and if it was roughly the same from each ear.'

'Sounds easy enough.' Nodding her head, GB1 then suddenly had a short coughing fit. Nurse Cheng immediately rushed over with a glass of water. The patient took it swiftly and drank most of it in one go.

'Alright?' inquired Lee.

'Yes, okay now,' said GB1, blowing her nose on a handkerchief. 'One of my everyday coughing fits.'

Lee placed the tuning fork in the charge box and waited for the green light. 'Here we go then,' he said, looking at the patient and holding the fork in front of her nose. The normal twenty seconds passed, and the fork continued to hum and vibrate. Lee took it away from the patient and hit it on the desk. It continued the humming for a further fifteen seconds. Lee stared at it with astonishment. 'Well I never, it's the first time it's been known to have a malfunction. Anyway, how was the sound to you?'

'Loud and clear,' said GB1. 'No difference between either ear.'

Lee nodded. 'Okay then, good. For the next test I will use the tuning fork again and hold it close to your ear while nipping your lower skull at the same time. Then the same procedure for the other ear.' Lee charged up the fork and later pulled it out of the box and placed it by the left ear of the patient while nipping the lower skull. 'Ouch', GB1 squealed softly. After twenty seconds Lee did the same to the other ear. Placing the fork on the table Lee smiled at GB1 and asked, 'Well, were both ears the same?'

'Yes,' replied GB1 flicking her hair back.

Lee looked at GB1 and said, 'One more test and then we are finished. I will whisper from a distance to see if you can hear what I am saying.'

'Alright,' nodded GB1.

Lee sat at the required distance and spoke. 'Number twenty-seven bus Orchard Road to Woodlands.'

GB1 thought for a couple of seconds and replied, 'Number twenty-seven bus Orchard Road to Woodlands.'

'That's completely correct,' smiled Lee. 'You can go now.'

Lee looked at Cheng and asked, 'Who is our last patient for ear testing?'

Cheng replied, 'It is going to be TW1, our twenty-one-year-old lady from Taiwan.' TW1 arrived on time carrying a flashy-looking shopping bag.

'Been shopping?' asked Lee.

'Yes, I bought a new dress,' laughed TW1. Cheng pointed to the patient's seat and TW1 quickly walked to it and sat down to make herself comfortable.

'We will do a few ear tests today. Have you any history of ear problems?' asked Lee.

'No, I have ok ears. Maybe once in my school days after swimming I got a little discomfort,' replied TW1.

'Yes, that is very common,' said Lee.

Lee did the same tests as the previous patients and concluded that TW1 had no ear issues.

CHAPTER 13

DAY THIRTEEN
DAY OUT AT THE BIRD PARK

The minibus pulled up outside the hospital.

Dr Aneleise Malinowski greeted the driver, who was a young, well-dressed man. He returned the greeting, 'Good afternoon, all ready for the Bird Park?' Malinowski looked at a clipboard she had in her hand, she ticked off the names and looked up to see who was present and ready to board the bus. She realised there was one patient missing, SG4. Malinowski looked all around her and the entrance door of the hospital. She then beckoned those waiting. 'Could you all get on the bus please?' Malinowski stood by the bus door for a few minutes and then got her mobile phone out and dialled the reception desk. 'Have you seen SG4 today? ... Oh so she is about, okay thanks Jenny.' Another few minutes went by then SG4 appeared, running from the hospital entrance.

'Doctor Malinowski,' she shouted. Malinowski waved and then welcomed her on the bus. Malinowski stopped at the top of the stairs by the driver.

'Okay, driver, we are all present. We have ten patients and me so eleven of us.' The driver nodded and started the bus. He then played with the radio before settling on a soft music channel.

The journey to Jurong took twenty-five minutes. The bus stopped outside the entrance gates, and everyone got off the bus. Malinowski pulled the tickets out of her bag. Looking to make sure all the group had got off, she counted the number of bodies. The driver remained seated and shouted, 'I'll be in the car park in about two hours' time for the return journey.'

'Lovely,' said Malinowski. She raised her arm. 'Right everybody. We will now go into the Bird Park and have our lunch before the organised tour.' Everyone followed Malinowski to the Songbird Terrace restaurant. A waitress greeted Malinowski with a smile.

'How many of you for lunch?'

'Eleven of us,' smiled Malinowski. The waiter showed the group to a nice outside table with parrots on trees nearby. After the group were seated the waitress took the drinks orders and left the table quickly. Ten minutes passed and two waitresses arrived with the drinks and one waitress had a parrot on her shoulder, squealing softly.

After all the drinks were on the table the head waitress said, 'The lunch will be ready in about fifteen minutes. Today's buffet lunch is fried chicken, tempura prawns, egg fried rice, and beef noodles.'

'Sounds great,' smiled Malinowski. The group chatted away happily. That is, except for SG3. He sat on very quietly and looked pale. He was sitting next to TW1 who asked about his wellbeing.

'I'm still under the weather. The Electric Shock Test seemed to have side effects. I have felt quite poorly since,' he snarled. TW1 placed hand of comfort on his shoulder.

'How many days ago was the test?'

'Er it will be a week tomorrow,' replied SG3. At that moment a parrot landed on his left shoulder and immediately made a loud noise and pooped. TW1 rolled around laughing at what had happened. SG3 raised a soft smile and said, 'Very nice, thank you very much, Mister Parrot.' A waitress had seen the episode and immediately rushed over and put her arm out and spoke to the parrot.

'Harry, you naughty boy. You are not supposed to poo on the customers.' Harry squawked. The waitress wiped the poo off SG3 with a paper towel.

The food arrived in great quantities, much to the delight of the party. After the initial tasting MK1 said, 'The tempura prawns are on a par with my restaurant in Malaysia, terrific.' SG2 slurped the beef noodles and managed to bring them to her mouth without losing any back in her bowl.

'The beef noodles are good, just like my mum's,' she said. The lunch went well with very little left over. The head waitress looked impressed at the consumption. She asked Dr. Malinowski if everyone was happy with the food.

'Delighted all round,' said Malinowski, giving her credit card to the waitress.

The tour guide arrived and everyone got to their feet and followed her. 'Welcome, everyone, to Jurong Bird Park. I have two buggies to take our party around the park. In that cart there, Jerry is waiting. I will drive the other so we will be split in to two groups.'

The sun shone all afternoon and the group returned to the ENT hospital in good spirits.

CHAPTER 14

DAY FOURTEEN
SUDDEN DEATH

HK1 sat uncomfortably in the chair of his room holding the left side below his rib cage. He gulped some water from a cup on the table. He then opened the cabinet door and took out a packet of indigestion tablets and quickly took three out of the silver wrapping and swallowed them. HK1 felt dizzy and shooting pains came and went in his chest. He started sweating profusely, even though the air con was turned up high. Jumping on to the bed, he wiped his forehead with a towel and shut his eyes. The breathing was indifferent, and he dozed off to sleep.

HK1 woke up with still the feeling of indigestion in his stomach. His chest was still hurting, and he sat up by the side of the bed and sighed. He picked up the phone on the side table and telephoned reception. 'Jenny, it's HK1 here, can I see a doctor? I am feeling terrible … I'm in my room … Okay I'll wait in my room for Doctor Tan.' Ten minutes passed and HK1 felt no better, then the door burst open, and Dr Audrey Tan walked in.

'What's the problem?' she asked.

'I feel lousy,' replied HK1. 'I feel like I have had indigestion since late last night. Also, I am getting chest pains coming and going, like shooting pains.' Tan sat down and looked at the patient.

'Anything else?'

'Yes, I am getting dizzy spells,' he answered.

Tan looked concerned and after a moment's thought she said, 'This is what we'll do. I'll give you some medication and you should rest for a few hours then I'll come back. You are not to smoke for the next few hours, and no coffee. Did you have breakfast?'

'Yes,' he replied. 'It was porridge, and it didn't seem to change the funny feeling in the stomach either way.' Tan walked to the door and looked back at the patient.

'Try and relax, I'll come back and see you later.'

'Thanks a lot,' said HK1 gratefully. After twenty minutes there was a knock at the door and then a nurse walked in with some tablets.

'Here are your painkillers, sir.' HK1 put his hand out and took the tablets from the nurse.

'Thanks for that,' he said. The nurse tidied up the bedside table and took away some rubbish.

'Is there anything else I can get you?' she asked.

'No, I'm fine,' replied HK1. The nurse departed and HK1 read the label on the bottle of tablets. Two tablets every two hours until the pain has subsided. HK1 grabbed a glass of water, half filling it. He swallowed the two required tablets and then laid on the bed and closed his eyes.

Three hours later Dr Audrey Tan returned and could see HK1 sleeping but he didn't look normal. His face was white and his breathing inconsistent. She shouted, 'HK1, HK1, HK1.' HK1 opened his eyes slowly.

'Where am I?' he said in shock. Tan held his hand.

'You are in your room. How are you feeling?' HK1 looked all around the room, a bit disorientated.

'I am still feeling rough. Very rough. The pains in my chest are quite intense. Something is wrong, I think.' Tan looked puzzled. HK1 let go of Tan's hand and sat up. 'I need the toilet,' he said, getting up from the bed. After five minutes in the toilet, he returned and sat in the chair by the bed. 'The pain is just terrible,' he complained. Then suddenly, he held his left side. 'Shit, what's happening, am I having a heart attack? I am having a heart attack.' He slumped in his chair, screaming in pain. 'Oh my god, oh my god. Oh my god.' Tan tried to grab him, but it was too late as he slumped to the floor, banging his head on the side table. He was dead.

Tan checked his pulse. 'Oh my god,' she shrieked. Standing up quickly she wiped her forehead with the back of her hand and picked up the phone in the room. 'Lee, disaster, HK1 has just had a heart attack his room and died … Okay will do.' Tan sat on the side of the bed and looked down at the dead patient. Five minutes passed and the door to the room opened quickly. Two porters with a stretcher and a blanket quickly lifted the dead HK1 on to the bed. They laid him flat on his back and covered his body and face with the blanket. They said nothing to Dr Tan, and she stood in silence as they wheeled the bed away.

Tan walked out of the room and headed for the office of Professor Lee. She knocked twice and walked in. Lee looked at her. 'Have a seat and tell me what happened.'

'Well, I got a distress call from HK1 around 2 p.m. this afternoon so I went to see him. He complained of indigestion and chest pains that were coming and going like daggers. Also, he complained of feeling dizzy. I prescribed some pain killers and told him to rest, I told him I would return in a few hours.' Lee looked puzzled.

'Were there any symptoms before today?'

'No, it's happened all of a sudden,' replied Tan. 'He had an unhealthy lifestyle, drinking and smoking heavily.' Lee turned to his computer and started typing.

'I'll send his wife an email asking when it's convenient to talk over the phone. We really didn't want this in the middle of a drugs trial.'

'Exactly,' agreed Tan. Lee finished typing and turned to look at Tan.

'So, you returned to the patient's room after a few hours?' Tan rolled her eyes.

'I returned at approximately five o' clock and found HK1 asleep. He heard me shouting his name and, after waking, complained of the same symptoms as before. After a brief period, he went to the bathroom. After around five minutes he returned still complaining of terrible pains in his chest. He sat in the chair and then held the left-hand side of his body. He fell part of the way down his chair and screamed he was having a heart attack. I tried to save him from falling on the floor but couldn't. He fell quickly and hit his head. And that was it.'

Lee wrote in his diary and looked up at Tan. 'Well Audrey I am so sorry you had to experience this awful event today. We have our weekly review tomorrow so I will see you then with developments. You will probably be interviewed by the police at some point.'

'Thanks Benjamin,' Tan said, leaving his office.

CHAPTER 15

DAY FIFTEEN
WEEK 2 REVIEW

Professor Lee entered the meeting room where he observed an almost full table and sat down with a small folder of notes. He shuffled the contents nervously. After a few minutes he looked at everyone sitting round the table. 'Who are we missing?' he asked. Dr Audrey Tan looked at Lee.

'We are just waiting for Dr Malinowski.'

'Okay I'll give her another five minutes and then start as we have a lot to go through today.' Five minutes passed and Dr Malinowski burst into the room apologising for her lateness.

Lee looked at everyone and then his notes. 'Welcome, everyone, to our week two review. It's been a really terrible week. I'll start with the sad death yesterday of our patient HK1. HK1 was a Hong Kong national, aged thirty-six years, and had five children. Yesterday he was feeling unwell, and Dr Tan answered a distress call in the early afternoon. And regrettably later in the afternoon he had a heart attack and fell to the floor and died instantly. His wife has been informed and will visit Singapore soon. Did anyone speak to HK1 in the last few days?'

ML1 raised his hand. 'Two days ago, I had a conversation with him and he told me that he had been to the Turf Club and lost a lot of money. He also got drunk and was violently sick before returning to the hospital.'

'Okay,' acknowledged Lee.

'Moving on.' He looked at his paperwork. 'The second terrible event to happen is that on day nine SG4 was having her throat examined and it was found to have a growth which is now known to be cancer. We would all like to say how sorry we are to hear this devastating news and hope the treatment in the near future at the General Hospital will be successful.' SG4 looked embarrassed but thanked Lee for his sympathetic words. Lee shuffled his notes and then cleared his throat. 'My third item is to do with SG3. We all know SG3 was the chosen patient to go on the Electric Shock Machine. He has had quite a few issues since the test and is not currently back to normal, so we wish him a quick recovery.' SG3 looked at Professor Lee.

'I am still not sleeping well and feeling very tired with aches and pains.'

Lee assured SG3, 'We will monitor your symptoms on a daily basis.' Lee poured himself a small glass of water from the table and gulped it quickly. 'Right, we move next to the patient review as per the same as last week. SG1, how has your week been?'

SG1 smiled. 'I have nothing to report, everything appears normal.'

'SG2 your situation please?'

'I also have nothing unusual to report.' Lee looked hard at SG3 who was looking miserable and coughed slightly.

'I already talked about my electric shock side effects but, on a positive note, I have not coughed quite as much as the first week. Maybe MK888 is helping, we'll see what happens next week.'

Lee smiled. 'Let's hope that it continues then. Next, er SG4, where are we now?'

SG4 flicked her hair nervously. 'Obviously I am waiting for cancer treatment but due to the fact it takes a while to set up, a number of weeks I think, I will be completing the MK888 experiment. Having missed the Ear Test recently I had an email to say I will have it now on day seventeen. As regards to my general situation, so far no known side effects to taking MK888. Therefore, happy to continue to the end.'

Lee said, 'Thanks for that update on your situation. I hope you get your treatment program started ASAP.'

SG5 coughed loudly and then had a coughing fit. Lee laughed, 'Carry on, you can cough as much as you like.'

'I'd rather not,' replied SG5, not appreciating the joke. 'Since I have been taking MK888 I have been sleeping quite badly. I normally get up in the night for the toilet several times, have done for many years, but now I am laying awake for several hours sometimes.'

Lee looked at his notes. 'Have you been taking any sleeping tablets?'

'Yes, but they don't seem to be working.'

Lee started writing and talking at the same time. 'Okay SG5. We will give you a different sleeping tablet to see if that helps.'

'Thanks,' said SG5.

Lee looked round the table and fixed his eyes on ML1. 'ML1 how's your week been?'

ML1 smiled. 'My week has been better than the previous. No stomach-ache to report. I had that three times last week after taking MK888 but this week no problem.' Lee nodded and then looked for the new patient

'ML2, how are you getting on?'

ML2 spoke softly. 'Actually, not great for me. I have been feeling a burning sensation after having a pee. Another thing is I had some discharge from both my eyes in the morning on two occasions.'

Lee made notes. 'Right, tomorrow you better have a blood test to see if we can find out what's wrong.'

'Yes, that sounds good,' smiled ML2.

Lee stared at GB1. 'Our British patient, what can you report?'

'I kept a record of headaches like you suggested last week,' said GB1, looking at a note in front of her. 'Day nine, no headache. Day ten, slight headache above the left eye. Day eleven, again minor headache above the left eye. Day twelve, bad headache central area of forehead. Day thirteen, no headache. Day fourteen. severe headache above left eye and today I had a minor headache above my left eye. All these headaches were roughly an hour to three hours after taking MK888.'

Lee wrote in his folder and then looked up. 'Pain is a mystery for us in the medical field. But because you are getting a lot of headaches, we'll give you a painkiller and see what happens.' GB1 nodded in agreement.

Lee looked tired, yawning slightly. 'Excuse me,' he said. 'Right, finally, TW1, what can you report in the last seven days?'

TW1 scratched her head nervously. 'I had been getting stomach-ache, maybe four days out of seven. This has happened soon after taking MK888.'

Lee stared at her. 'Did you get this in week one?'

'No, I didn't. In week one my coughing situation was

slightly worse than normal. And week two my coughing is roughly back to pre-MK888 levels.' Lee thought for a moment then looked at Dr Malinowski. 'I'll get Dr Malinowski to sort you out some medication for that.' Malinowski nodded in agreement. 'Okay so we have done our patient reviews for the week. I just want to let everyone know what is coming up this week. Day sixteen we will be doing CT scans for everyone. This is quite painless and, if you haven't already experienced it, I'll just let you know that you lay on a bed and go under a donut-looking object. Before the test you are given something to drink which will help with the images of your body. The scan takes around twenty-five minutes and it's unlikely that you get any side effects, other than the taste of metal in your mouth. We will do all the CT scans in the morning so nobody must eat or drink anything tomorrow morning. You can only drink water until after you have had your test. On day eighteen everyone will be having a food intolerance test. It should be quite interesting. Then on day nineteen we will be having an alcohol drinks test. That should be fun too! So, I think a week to look forward to. Any problems along the way, email or phone the medical team for help. Anyone got any questions?' Lee looked around the room and ML2 put her hand up.

'I have a small problem with the tap on my basin.'

Lee replied, 'If you have a word with Jenny on reception, she will get one of the maintenance people to fix it.' Lee tidied his papers and left the room, followed by all the others.

CHAPTER 16

DAY SIXTEEN
CT SCANS

ML2 sat in the small treatment room waiting for Nurse Cheng to come and take her blood. The room was painted the traditional magnolia creamy white. Small paintings of Singapore hung on the walls. Nurse Cheng arrived, smiling sweetly. 'How are you today?' she said.

ML2 hesitated. 'A little under the weather. I keep getting a burning sensation after a visit to the bathroom.'

'Oh dear' Cheng remarked. 'It might be an infection. Right, I'll take a small blood sample and then you can go.' Cheng took the blood sample and ML2 stood up, holding her arm. Cheng told her to go to Dr Malinowski's office at four o' clock the same day to get the results.

Over in the massive X-ray room the CT Scanning was underway. SG1 took a sip of the coloured liquid he had been given and then lay on the bed. Dr Wong set up the machine, ready for the test.

'What's that drink like?'

'Not great,' replied SG1. 'I'd rather have a beer.' Wong laughed.

'During the test I will be next door. I can see you so if there is any problem just raise your arm at anytime. During the test if you can keep as still as possible.' Wong disappeared and the scanner soon started with a gentle hum. The time went quickly and SG1 enjoyed the experience apart from the taste of the drink.

The next patient to arrive was SG2. She looked at the scanner and remarked, 'It's a bit different from an MRI scanner.'

Wong confirmed, 'It's less daunting because you don't have to go into a tunnel. You'll just be looking at a donut above where you lay. If you would like to lay on the bed. Sorry, take this drink first. Sometime after the scan you may taste metal in your mouth. This is normal.' SG2 placed the beaker of coloured liquid in the holder by the bed. The patient laid down and Wong made the pillow under her head more comfortable. 'Right, I will operate the machine from the room next door. If you have any problems, then please raise your hand at any time. During the test try to stay as still as possible.'

After the test Wong rushed in and asked if the patient was okay. 'Fine, no problem,' said SG2.

Wong smiled. 'I thought you went to sleep as you were so still.'

SG2 said, 'I may have dozed off for a few minutes.

The next patient to arrive was SG3, his multi-coloured hair flipping behind him as he walked. Wong greeted him. 'Are you alright?'

'I'm half left,' said SG3. Wong went through the motions with the patient slowly. SG3 looked a bit out of it throughout. Glazed eyes and fidgety. Twice during the test Wong had to ask him to lay still. SG4 arrived ten minutes late and apologised emphatically. Wong pointed to the seat next to the scanner. 'I was sorry to hear of your cancer.'

'Yes it hit me for six. Hopefully I get through to the other side,' said SG4.

'What stage is it at?' asked Wong.

'I think stage one, so that's something,' said SG4. Wong gave the standard intro to the patient. After the scan was finished Wong asked SG4 about her work as a lawyer. They chatted away for a while before Wong realised that time was overdue for the next patient.

Wong picked up the phone and telephoned Dr Audrey Tan. 'Audrey hi, Fu here, I'm just doing SG5, the fifth patient on the CT scan … Can you do the next four? … Okay that's great, thank you.' Wong returned to the CT scanner where SG5 was just taking the coloured drink. 'How's the drink? Wong asked.

SG5 smiled. 'I wouldn't want it every day.'

Wong laughed. 'Lucky you don't have to. That drink helps the images become clearer.'

'How many images will you take on a CT scan?' SG5 asked.

'Oh, it's about one thousand two hundred,' replied Wong. SG5 took up position and laid on the bed. Wong asked if the patient was comfortable. SG5 nodded. Wong said. 'Okay I'll be next door and return in about twenty minutes after the scan has finished.' The scan went smoothly and SG5 left the room in good spirits.

Wong opened the door and peeped at the waiting area just down the corridor. One rather fat man was the only patient waiting. Wong shouted, 'ML1.' The man got up quickly.

'Coming, coming,' he shrieked. Wong pointed to the chair by the bed and read the script as before with the previous patients. 'Dr Audrey Tan will be doing your test and should be with us shortly.' At this point Dr Tan walked in the room. Greetings were exchanged and the patient took the coloured drink and laid on the bed. Wong and Tan left for the control room next door for a five-minute chat. Then Wong left and Tan carried out the scanning test. It went well for ten minutes then the machine cut out. Tan looked at the computer for an error message but could not see any. She scratched her head, then walked next door to speak to ML1. 'Sorry, the CT machine has malfunctioned.' ML1 sat up on the bed.

'Oh, I see.' Tan inspected the machine all around and then felt the 'donut' part at the top.

'My god, that's hot,' she exclaimed. 'We will have to let it cool down and then try again.' Tan waited half an hour and felt the donut again. It had cooled sufficiently and the CT scan was then carried out successfully.

ML2 arrived dressed impressively. Dr Tan looked at her patient, admiring her clothes. 'Nice dress,' she remarked.

'Thank you,' blushed ML2. 'Bought in Takamashayer.' Dr Tan went through the procedure for the CT scan and then, having the patient ready, walked towards the door to the next room and then looked back.

'Fingers crossed the scanner goes okay. The last patient had to have two scans because the first time the scanner overheated.' The scan went well this time, to the relief of Dr Tan.

GB1 arrived in a coughing fit. 'Sorry,' she apologised.

Dr Tan said, 'That's why we are here, to solve the coughing problem.'

'Indeed,' said GB1. After Tan read the script of the CT Scan, she felt the donut on the machine and it felt a little warm.

'Now we should wait a little longer as the scanner has been running a little hot.'

'Sure,' agreed GB1.

Tan smiled at the patient. 'I hope to have a holiday next

year in your country.'

'Actually, I don't consider the UK as my country. I was born in Singapore and hardly spent any time in the UK. Yes, probably only a few weeks of my twenty-nine years have been in the UK.'

'Really?' said Tan, surprised.

'My father and mother moved here when they were quite young and had an export/import business and an antique shop which I now run,' GB1 said.

'That's interesting,' said Tan. 'And whereabouts do you live in Singapore?'

GB1 smiled, 'We are quite lucky, we live in Emerald Hill off Orchard Road. I have a Singaporean husband and his grandmother gave us the house. In fact, it's two houses knocked in to one so we have great living space and a large garden.'

'Wonderful,' shrieked Tan.

GB1 said, 'Maybe you'd like to come round and see it.?'

'Yes, I'd love that,' replied Tan.

GB1 thought for a moment. 'I'll be popping home on day twenty-one. Could you come for lunch?'

'Yes, I'd like that,' said Tan, delighted.

GB1 nodded. 'Okay we'll walk there together from here; it will only take us ten minutes.'

'Great, I look forward to it,' Tan confirmed.

The final patient arrived thirty minutes later. 'Sorry, sorry,' TW1 squealed. 'I totally lost track of time today.'

'No worries,' said Tan. 'The CT machine has been getting a bit hot and bothered today so it's had time to cool down before your scan takes place.' Tan carried out the scan and said goodbye to TW1.

Meanwhile, in Dr Malinowski's office, ML2 had arrived to get the results of her blood test. Dr Malinowski looked serious. 'How are you feeling?'

ML2 pointed to her eyes. 'A bit of discomfort there and also when using the bathroom.'

'I have to ask, how is your sex life?'

Taken aback, ML2 replied. 'Well, it's good although not regular.' Malinowski scratched her face.

'How many sexual partners in the last month?' ML2 thought for a moment.

'I have had sex with three different men.'

Malinowski shook her head. 'Well from one or more of those guys you have picked up an infection.'

'VD?' asked ML2, horrified.

'I'm afraid so,' confirmed Malinowski. 'But not one, you've got two.'

'Oh my god,' shrieked ML2. Malinowski looked down at her notes.

'You have Chlamydia and Gonorrhoea. Now a course of antibiotics will clear it up within seven days. I am also giving you eye drops to ease the discomfort there.'

'Thanks,' said ML2, still shocked at the things she was hearing. Malinowski looked unhappy with the patient.

'If it's possible, can you contact the three men you had sex with and let them know your situation? It's important as it might stop the spread.'

'I'll do that, no problem,' said ML2.

CHAPTER 17

DAY SEVENTEEN
MISSING PATIENT

Jenny was sitting at reception working on the computer when the head cleaner walked up to the desk. 'Can I just inform you that SG3 seems to have gone. His room is empty of all belongings and his bed was not slept in last night.'

'Oh, that's strange. Well, thanks for letting me know,' said Jenny, looked puzzled. Immediately she picked up the phone and dialled Professor Lee. 'Professor Lee, Jenny here. It appears that SG3 has discharged himself from the hospital. The head cleaner said his room has no personal items and the bed was not slept in last night … Okay.' Jenny placed the phone down and went back to typing on the computer.

Lee jumped from his office and stormed down the corridor to check SG3's room. He looked in the wardrobe and bedside cabinet. Nothing. Lee shook his head in amazement. He then stormed back to his office and sat down by the computer, he looked for contact details of the missing patient. Lee dialled the mobile phone number, no answer. He dialled the apartment, no answer. Frustrated, Lee went back to the computer to look for family contacts. Lee found a mobile number for the father of the patient. Lee dialled quickly; he got an answer. 'Peter, it's Professor Lee at the Singapore ENT Hospital. As you know your son has been participating in an experiment here to trial a new drug. It looks like he has discharged himself without telling anyone … Have you not seen him? … Oh, I see. Well, if he comes home can you let me know? Great, thank you Peter.'

In the treatment room SG4 was with Dr Wong having the ear tests that she had missed while taking time out with her cancer treatment planning. Wong went through the details. 'Have you any previous ear problems?'

'No I have never suffered any ear issues.'

Wong smiled. 'As for today it will be just a few simple tests and I will look into each ear with a device to make sure everything looks normal, okay?' The fork tests were normal, as was the whisper test. Wong used the otoscope thoroughly and discovered some wax. 'You have some wax in the right ear, I will ask Pharmacy to provide you with ear drops that should help get rid of it. It's not bad enough to have it syringed out.'

Professor Lee stood at the arrivals part of the airport, waiting for Mrs Chow to arrive. He was not looking forward to the arrival of HK1's wife. HK1 had previously told Lee that his wife was fiery. Coming to Singapore for a month was a nice break for him and he could relax without the constant earbashing. Mind you, HK1 had hardly been a good husband. He drank most of the time and gambled away large sums of money. Having not met Mrs Chow before, Lee did not know what she looked like, so he held up a card with his name in black bold type, Professor Benjamin Lee. Many passengers went by and then Lee noticed an attractive woman in white wave in his direction. She hurried herself towards him. 'Professor Lee.' Lee smiled and took her suitcase.

'Welcome to Singapore, Mrs Chow.' Mrs Chow half smiled as she did not look in a good mood. Lee looked at her as they walked to the exit area. 'I'll just make a quick call, and someone will bring my car to the front of the terminal.'

Lee stopped and pulled his phone from his shirt pocket. He dialled the valet services. After the call he put the phone back in his pocket. 'Five minutes for the car, Mrs Chow.' Chow began waking again.

'You can call me Tasmin.' Lee walked with her stride for stride.

'I am Benjamin. Oh, I forgot it's on the card I held up,' said Lee, a little embarrassed. They reached the exit doors and walked out towards valet waiting area. The front of the airport was busy with taxis and buses and people everywhere. Five minutes passed and Lee's BMW arrived, a young man got out. 'Professor Lee?' he called.

'That's me,' replied Lee. The young driver took Mrs Chow's suitcase and placed it neatly in the boot. Then he walked over to Lee. 'There are your keys, sir.'

'Thanks,' said Lee and he got in his car. Chow was seconds behind him and got in the passenger's side. Lee drove fast and they arrived at the ENT hospital inside twenty minutes. Lee parked his car in the reserved parking space and ran round the other side of the car to open the door for Mrs Chow. He then opened the boot and removed Mrs Chow's suitcase. 'I'll leave your suitcase in reception and then after our chat I'll get you a taxi to take you to your hotel,' said Lee.

'That's great, thanks,' said Chow.

Lee asked, 'What hotel are you staying at?'

Chow replied., 'Raffles Hotel.' They walked into the hospital reception and Lee left the suitcase with Jenny to look after.

Lee and Chow walked to his office and sat down. 'Tasmin, would you like a drink?' Lee asked.

'A Chinese tea would be nice, thank you.' Chow replied. Lee picked up the phone and spoke to the kitchen.

'Could I have a pot of Chinese tea and two cups in my office, please? Thank you very much.' Lee had a more serious look on his face. 'Okay let's go through what happened with your husband. Well, to give you the medical aspect of your husband's heart attack, this was an STEM1 heart attack, which is the worst you can have. With this kind of heart attack the main heart artery is one hundred per cent blocked whereas typically a heart attack without instant death would have a partial blocked artery.'

Mrs Chow listened closely. 'I see,' she said. Lee heard his mobile buzz on. He picked it up from the desk and read the text and then put it down again. 'Right, where were we? Yes three days ago, late morning your husband complained of chest pains and dizziness. Dr Audrey Tan went to see him in his room. He was found to be very unwell. Dr Tan told him to relax and that she would return a few hours later to check on his condition. In the meantime, Dr Tan would ask Pharmacy to provide him with painkillers. Dr Tan went back to see your husband mid afternoon and found him asleep but breathing badly and he looked very white faced. Tan had to shout quite loudly to get him to wake up. Eventually he opened his eyes and complained of darting chest pains. He used the toilet and, when he returned, he sat in the chair for a moment. And then complained that he thought he was having a heart attack. He tried to get up and slumped to the floor and hit his head and died.'

Mrs Chow shook her head. 'He had been a heavy drinker and smoker all the time we were together. I think his lifestyle has not been healthy. Never healthy really.' The door opened and a kitchen worker brought a tray in with the Chinese tea.

'Leave it on the side table, thanks,' said Lee. After they were alone again Lee continued. 'Er your husband had been to the Singapore Turf Club the night before his death and had lost a lot of money. He told one of the other patients here.'

Chow snapped. 'He's been a bastard, always wasting money on horse racing. We had numerous rows on the subject. Once he lost a million Hong Kong dollars in one night at the casino. I thought he was visiting his brother and I found a hotel receipt in his trousers. He had been to Macau for a massive gambling binge. We almost got divorced over it.'

Lee looked away and then back at Chow. 'It's a triple whammy, drinking, smoking, and gambling. Do you think his coughing was related to smoking?'

'Well, if you do anything bad to excess then there will be a bad result.' Lee poured out the tea and picked up a cup and offered it to Chow. Chow took the cup. 'Thanks.' Chow continued, 'Yes, my husband smoked from an early age. It was the fashion in days gone by. A big social thing. You bought someone a drink and then offered them a cigarette at the same time. Tony started smoking very early. I think from maybe aged thirteen.'

'Really?' said Lee, surprised.

'Yes, very young, and I think he tried all types. The strong French ciggies, the coloured Turkish variety. Oh, and he went through a period before we met when cigars were his thing. Huge long Cubans he told me. Must have cost a fortune.'

'Interesting,' said Lee. 'What about his general diet, did he eat a lot of rubbish?'

Chow nodded her head. 'Yep, he probably had too much batter in his diet. Spring rolls, fried chicken, sticky ribs, and not forgetting sweet and sour pork.' They paused for a moment and drank some tea. Lee looked at his computer briefly, glancing over his emails, and then turned to Chow.

'How many nights are you spending in Singapore?' Chow replied.

'Just two. I'm meeting my cousin tomorrow night. She is working for a property company in Wisma Atria.' Lee looked down to the floor and then up.

'When will you come back here to collect your husband's belongings?'

Chow looked serious. 'I'll give you a call, it'll probably be the day after tomorrow.'

'That's fine,' said Lee. 'I have to see a patient soon, so I'll walk with you to reception and ask Jenny to get you a taxi to Raffle's Hotel.' They wished each other goodbye in the reception area.

In the library a workman was repairing a broken bookcase. It had fallen and damaged one side. Nurse Cheng picked up a number of books that had fallen out and placed them on a table. The workmen held the bookcase up and smiled at Cheng.

'If you want to take the rest off, I'll hold it for a while.'

'Yes, thanks,' she said gratefully. After tidying up the books Cheng thought out loud, 'Now I've forgotten what book I came to look for, urgh.'

CHAPTER 18

DAY EIGHTEEN
FOOD INTOLERANCE TESTS

Malinowski and Cheng were in the treatment room preparing everything for the day's Food Intolerance Tests. Cheng was feeling exhausted after labelling all the sample tubes she had prepared for each of the eight patients. Malinowski looked at everything on the tables and checked everything to a clipboard meticulously. 'Now is there anything missing here, ah, what about the scissors for cutting the hair sample?' Cheng quickly went to a drawer and pulled out and held up to her colleague two pairs of scissors. Malinowski looked pleased. 'That's it then, we are ready to go.' Cheng gave the tables another glance and fixed her gaze on the BER machine which was the size of a typical microwave.

'Have we tested the BER machine is working?'

'No let's do that,' she said. 'You can be the patient and I'll be the doctor.' Cheng pulled up a chair next to the BER machine and Malinowski did the same the other side of the table. They ran the machine for five minutes and it appeared to be in good order. Cheng was a bit concerned with some of the results.

'Rice, pork, tuna intolerances. I cannot believe it.'

Malinowski giggled. 'You don't want to believe it.'

SG1 looked on astonished at all the tubes, containers, bottles etc as ~~she~~ he sat on the treatment bed. Nurse Cheng smiled at SG1. 'Took me ages to get all that lot together.'

'I bet,' said SG1. Dr Malinowski walked over to SG1 and sat next to the treatment bed.

'How are you?'

SG1 answered. 'I'm good, looks like it could be an interesting day.' Malinowski looked at her notes and then up to the patient.

'Today is quite busy. We will do four things. One is a finger prick blood test where we get the results another day. Two is a hair sample test where we get the results another day. Three is a skin prick test where we get the results immediately. Test four is the BER machine where the results are immediate.'

'Sounds interesting,' smiled SG1.

'I cannot guarantee you'll enjoy all of it but just try and relax and we'll find out what might be bad for you. For test one Nurse Cheng will prick your finger slightly and put the sample on a slide to be analysed later.' Malinowski got up from the chair and Cheng replaced her with a small needle and a small slide. Cheng looked at SG1.

'Are we ready then?'

SG1's smile disappeared. 'I'm ready.' It only took a few seconds and SG1 held a small piece of cotton wool over the spot where the blood sample had been taken. Cheng moved to the worktop on the side and placed the patient sample neatly in a corner. Meanwhile, Malinowski sat down next to the patient. 'Now I'm going to give you a haircut.'

'Don't take too much,' SG1 joked. Malinowski picked up the scissors.

'No, only a spoon's worth.' Malinowski placed the hair sample in a small plastic container.

Cheng arrived with a small gadget for the forthcoming

Prick Test. 'Now this next test is probably the worst but it's bearable. I'll be pricking your left arm twice and your right arm twice so if you would like to roll the sleeves up of your shirt.' SG1 immediately prepared himself for what lay ahead.

'What will the four tests refer to?' asked SG1. Cheng smiled as she did the first prick.

'This first one is dairy, the second meats, the third is fish, and the fourth vegetables.' Cheng pulled the gadget away from the patient. 'How's that feel?'

'Not too bad,' SG1 replied.

'If a rash or deep redness appears then you have an intolerance.' Cheng did the second prick on the left arm. Moving on to the right arm Cheng did the third and fourth test in quick succession. After a few moments, the Prick Test number three for fish seemed to create a deep red blotch. 'Oh dear,' said Cheng, staring at the right arm. 'It would appear you may have a problem with fish.'

'Really?' said SG1, surprised. 'It's stinging quite badly.' Cheng turned to look at Malinowski sitting on a computer at another desk.

'Dr Malinowski, we have a fish reaction.' Malinowski looked at Cheng.

'That's interesting, I wonder what type though, that's the sixty-four-million-dollar question.'

Cheng swung around in the chair and looked at SG1. 'We will give the tests ten minutes to see the reaction.'

The ten minutes passed, and no additional reactions came to light 'So will I have to stop eating fish?' asked SG1.

Cheng replied. 'It will be advised once we have finished the course in this hospital. You will be getting a number of recommendations. As regards food intolerances, you will cut out certain foods for three months and then return here for an analysis of how your system has reacted.'

Malinowski prepared for the BER test. After a few minutes she handed the black torch to SG1. 'Hold that please,' she demanded. Grabbing the other torch Malinowski smiled widely. 'Ready to go. If you should hear a loud beep, it means a certain food or drink is possibly bad for you.' SG1 nodded.

'How many different things are you testing for?' Malinowski looked at the patient seriously.

'Over one hundred food and drink items.' The test was carried out and the only negatives were pineapple, almonds, hazelnuts, and lobster.

SG1 left the room and Malinowski carried the BER machine to the computer desk and connected it to the computer and made some notes. After a short time, she carried the machine back to the table near the patient's treatment bed. The second patient for testing arrived slightly out of breath. Malinowski looked at her. 'What have you been doing?'

'I have been out for a run. I ran from Boat Quay to Orchard Road and now I am exhausted.'

Cheng smiled at SG2. 'We'll let you get your breath back and then we'll start the tests.' Cheng filled in SG2 about the various tests. SG2 got her breath back and the first two tests passed quickly. On to the third test and SG2 rolled up her sleeves. 'This will be interesting. I always thought I might have a dairy problem.'

'Why's that?' asked Cheng.

SG2 scratched her head. 'I seem to have a coughing fit after drinking coffee with milk, but if I drink it black then I am alright. Also, I've known food containing cheese can give me stomach-ache.' Cheng looked at SG2 closely and held up the gadget.

'Let's see then.' Cheng pricked her left arm and then quickly changed the cartridge and found another spot on the arm to prick it again. 'That's dairy and meat tests.' Before Cheng had time to do prick three, the first one – the dairy test – created a reddening of the spot that was pricked.

'Ooh, I am getting a tingling on that first one,' said SG2 alarmed.

'Yes, that is the dairy intolerance test,' nodded Cheng. 'Let's do the fish and vegetable tests on your other arm.' Cheng did the final two prick tests without a reaction.

Malinowski switched on the BER machine. SG2 looked at it with amazement. 'It looks like a microwave.'

Malinowski laughed out loud. 'Its official name is Bioenergetics Response Machine. Designed and made in Germany.' Malinowski fixed all the attachments and held out a black device that looked like a torch. 'You'll be holding that while I continuously press your other hand with another little device. I then see a flashing red light on the box if there is a problem.'

'Amazing technology,' said SG2. 'And how accurate is it?' she added.

Malinowski thought for a minute then replied, 'Around seventy-five per cent. If you like to hold the torch in your left hand, I will start the test by prodding the right hand with the other device, okay?' Malinowski started the test and every couple of minutes there was a bleep, bleep sound.

'Can I ask how many items are being tested?' said SG2.

Malinowski stopped the test for a moment. 'I think it's over one hundred.' The test was completed, and Malinowski took the black torch off the patient. 'Well, I can see a few negatives come up. Mainly fruit and grain types of food. Oh, and chocolate was a strong negative. Do you like eating chocolate?'

'Yes I do, quite a lot,' said SG2 with a disappointed look on her face. Malinowski carried the machine to the computer desk and plugged it in to her PC and then walked back to the patient.

'The machine will produce a report which I will email to you,' explained Malinowski.

'I will look forward to receiving that,' said SG2, preparing herself to leave the treatment room.

SG4 took up position ready for her food intolerances tests. She closed her eyes for a moment and then opened them. 'Feeling tired?' Cheng asked. SG4 nodded.

'Yes, I am not sleeping well, now I know I have throat cancer.'

'Must be a very difficult period for you,' Cheng said sympathetically. SG4 rolled up the sleeves of her blouse, ready for the tests.

'I should get to know the start date of my treatment program soon. I hope I don't have to have radiotherapy as well as chemotherapy.'

'Yes the radiotherapy can be tough, sometimes five days a week up to two months.'

'Really?' sighed SG4.

Cheng fixed the device for the first test. 'Okay so we'll get started then. Number one test is where I prick your finger with this little gadget here and put a small amount of blood on a slide to be analysed.' Cheng did the test quickly. 'Right, that's done, while I deal with that Dr Malinowski will take a small amount of hair to go to the lab for testing.' Cheng took the slide to the worktop area and Malinowski sat down next to SG4. She held up a pair of small scissors.

'Just a small piece of hair for the lab.'

'Okay then,' laughed SG4. Malinowski placed the hair in a little tube and carried it over to the worktop and gave it to Cheng to place neatly in the lab tray.

Cheng skipped back to the patient and asked about her wellbeing. SG4 confirmed she was feeling fine. Cheng picked up the device for skin prick test. 'Okay here we go with test three. I will be pricking your skin in four places. Two on the left arm and two on the right arm. We have four groups here. Dairy, meats, fish, and vegetables. Now, if you have an intolerance for any of these groups your skin will go red very quickly and you may experience an itchy irritation.'

SG4 looked at her arm before the tests started. 'Sounds interesting. How accurate are these tests?

'They are not a hundred per cent but if there's a strong intolerance it will show up. So, let's go then. Hold out your left arm straight. First one is dairy and I will then do meats.' Cheng did the two tests and held the patient's arm for a moment. Cheng let go of her hand. 'Relax.' A minute or two went by. Cheng asked. 'Feel anything?'

'Nope,' replied SG4. Cheng did the tests on the right arm.

'Okay, the two I just did, one is for fish and the other for general vegetables.' The patient and nurse stared at the tiny marks on the arms. Minutes went by. Nothing happened. 'Looks like there is no problem according to those tests,' said Cheng.

'What's next?' inquired SG4.

'Next will be the BER machine test which Dr Malinowski will do shortly.'

Malinowski carried the machine over to the table near the patient. 'This wonderful box is the BER machine, designed in Germany. This machine is supposed to tell us what your body does not like.'

'Very interesting, I've heard of this system before,' said SG4. Malinowski switched on the machine and handed the black torch to SG4.

'Well in this hospital we are trying to look at the problems with more than one type of testing. If you just hold that torch steady and I will use another gadget to continually touch your other hand. The machine will give me a green light or red light depending on if there is a certain food problem. Okay I am ready now, let's see what we get.' For the first ten minutes all the results were green and then the red light showed. It showed bright and the machine buzzed loudly.

Malinowski looked at SG4. 'Ah ha, we have a bad one.'

'What is it?' asked SG4 loudly.

'It is white wine,' replied Malinowski. 'Do you drink much white wine?'

'Not that often,' replied SG4. 'Mostly I drink red wine.' Malinowski looked at her reading on the machine.

'Red wine is fine. Strange. Okay we'll press on with the other categories.' Minutes went by and everything was green then a red approved. 'Onions no good,' Malinowski said, looking at the patient. The next few were fine then another red followed by two more red flashes. 'Right those three reds in a row are all fruit – apricots, blackcurrant, and honey.' SG4 shook her head from side to side. The rest of the test went with no more reds.

SG5 arrived in the treatment room with a horrendous coughing fit. Cheng filled a glass with water quickly and handed it to SG5. He took it gratefully with a shaking hand and drank half of it, spilling some on his shirt. 'Thanks a million,' he gasped.

'That was some coughing fit,' added Malinowski.

'Yes I do have them,' complained SG5. 'I need more MK888.' Cheng asked if he would like more water. He shook his head and sat back in the chair.

'Will you be okay for the tests today? Cheng asked.

'I think so,' he said, rolling up the sleeves of his shirt and using a piece of tissue to dry the water he had spilled. Cheng talked through the forthcoming tests and SG5 felt relaxed and happy with what was to come.

Tests one and two passed quickly and when the third test was about to start SG5 scratched his head. 'I think I had this test once before and got a red blotch and irritation immediately. But I cannot remember which category hit the hay.'

'Let's find out, shall we?' said Cheng, preparing the skin prick machine. 'So I am going to prick your skin twice on each arm and we are looking for a reaction to dairy, meats, fish, and veg. There is no discomfort unless you have a problem with these categories. And only then will you get a redness and irritation on the skin, okay?' Cheng did the three tests and no redness appeared. Almost immediately after the fourth test the skin went red and began to swell.

'I have a tingle, a big tingle from that one,' complained SG5. Cheng looked at him.

'That is the vegetable one which is quite rare.' SG5 rolled down his shirt and did up the buttons.

He stared at Cheng. 'Ah but which veg is bad for me?'

'Not so easy, that question will require further tests,'

laughed Cheng. 'Maybe the BER machine will tell us.'

Malinowski took up the seat next to the patient and prepared the BER machine. She handed the black torch to the patient. 'You need to hold that black torch throughout. I will be prodding your other hand continually and looking at the machine to observe either a green light or a red light. The greens are good, and the reds means you have an intolerance with that particular food or drink item.' Twenty minutes passed and all symbols were showing green. As the test moved on to individual vegetables the situation changed. The machine vibrated and hummed, and three vegetables showed red. Malinowski turned to SG5. 'Here we are, it seems a problem with potatoes, broccoli, and onions.'

'I don't like the sound of that,' said SG5, disappointed. The remainder of the test only found one other red category which was lager beer.

ML1 arrived smiling happily and took the patient's seat. 'Why are you so happy?' asked Cheng.

ML1 smiled widely. 'I just won the Singapore Sweep.'

'Really, how much?' Cheng demanded to know.

'Five thousand dollars,' shrieked ML1.

'I thought you were gonna say two million dollars,' Cheng commented a little disappointed.

'Well I'm quite happy with five grand. I can have a nice family holiday with that,' said ML1. He continued. 'One of my customers won half a million a few years ago. He paid for a weekend break for me and my wife in Genting Highlands. Lovely it was.'

Cheng prepared for the first test. 'Okay sir. I will just take a finger and prick it and put the blood on a slide to be analysed. There we are, done already!' ML1 looked at his finger and then looked away. Cheng got up from the chair with the slide. 'While I deal with this, Dr Malinowski will just take a sample of your hair to be sent to the laboratory.'

ML1 rolled his eyes. 'Never thought a hair sample could be of medical assistance.'

Cheng turned her head to one side. 'It's a medical view that hair sample can show any adverse effect of a new drug. So, while the patients here are taking MK888, we want to see if there are any deficiencies or changes to normal body systems – hormonal, immune, neutron transmitters.'

'Most interesting,' nodded. ML1.

Malinowski arrived with a pair of scissors. ML1 joked, 'Don't take too much, I don't have a lot of hair.'

'I only need a few strands, believe me.' The hair sample was taken, and Malinowski took it away to prepare for the lab. Cheng retired and sat down next to the patient.

'If you could please roll up the sleeves of both arms. I am going to prick your skin four times, twice on each arm.'

'And what's that for?' asked ML1.

'It's to discover if you have any problems with dairy, meats, fish, and vegetables. Have you had such a test previously?'

'No, I don't recall such a test,' replied ML1.

'Okay so, I will now prick your skin on your arm, first arm for dairy and meats. If there is an intolerance your skin will swell and go red immediately around the area where I made the prick.'

'I see,' said the patient. Cheng did the first two tests, and nothing amiss came to light. On the other arm a small reaction developed on the fish category and a large reaction developed on the vegetables. 'So am I now to give up eating fish and vegetables?' the patient quizzed Cheng.

'No, it's not that straight forward. In a moment Dr Malinowski will do the final test today which is on a BER machine. That will tell us which fish and vegetables your system does not like.'

Malinowski took up position next to the patient and set up BER machine. 'Now this is the intolerance. This wonderful box here will tell me which individual foods don't suit you. If you hold this black torch-like device while I will prod your other hand and look for either a green light if okay and a red light if there is a problem.'

ML1 smiled. 'Fascinating, absolutely fascinating!' The test started and some ten minutes passed before the machine vibrated and bleeped loudly. Malinowski stared at the box.

'Ah hah we have a red and it's prawn.' ML1 made no comment and the test continued for some time before the machine bleeped again. Malinowski looked ML1. 'Right, we have another three red lights. They are peas, broccoli, and onions. Don't worry, everyone has some intolerances these days. Sometimes cutting this out of the diet for a few months can help the body recover.' ML1 sat deep in thought and scratched his neck, he made no comments. The test was complete with no further negatives.

ML2 arrived and left a trail of fragrant perfume from the entrance door to the treatment bed. Cheng and Malinowski looked at each other, sensing each other's thoughts. Cheng went through the procedures with the patient and quickly carried out the first two. Cheng smiled at ML2. 'Now we get more interesting. I will prick your skin four times to see if you have any intolerance with dairy, meat, fish, or vegetables.'

'Will there be any blood?' asked ML2.

Cheng replied quickly, 'No, I only just touch the skin surface with my gadget here. The response is immediate. If you have a problem with a category your skin will go very red very quickly and may swell up. But the discomfort will only be small, so don't worry.' Cheng carried out the four tests and no reaction was seen on the patient's skin.

Malinowski handed ML2 the torch and started the BER test. After twenty minutes of no red lights there was suddenly a row of reds in the nuts categories. Peanuts, almonds, walnuts, and hazelnuts all showed red on the machine. Malinowski turned to ML2. 'Have you ever had a reaction from eating nuts?'

'Yes,' replied ML2. 'I often cough soon after eating nuts or foods with an element of nuts in them.'

'Really?' commented Malinowski. The rest of the test was mainly positive but red lights flashed on white wine, vodka, caramel, and cigarette smoke.

GB1 sat down in the patient's chair and Cheng smiled at her while getting the first test ready. 'How is it going?' she asked.

'It's fine,' replied GB1. 'I don't seem to be getting the headaches I did in the first two weeks.'

'That's good,' said Cheng, picking up the first prick gadget. 'I will just gently prick your skin and place the blood sample on a slide. This will then be analysed in the laboratory.' GB1 held out her hand, flinched slightly, and her finger was pricked. Cheng gave the patient a small piece of gauze to hold in the area where the prick was made. Malinowski arrived with the scissors.

'Ready for a little haircut?' GB1 looked surprised.

'A hair sample, what is the reason behind that then?'

Malinowski cut a small piece of hair from the patient. 'It can tell us if the medication the patient is taking is having any adverse effect on their health.'

'I never knew that.' Malinowski took the hair sample away and placed it in a container.

Cheng returned to sit near the patient. 'Now we move on to test three, which is the skin prick test. If you could remove your cardigan so your arms are exposed, I will prick each arm twice.'

'What will that do?' asked GB1. Cheng stopped preparing for a moment.

'This will tell us if you have any problems with dairy, meats, fish, or vegetables. After I have pricked your skin there could be an immediate reaction when your skin tingles and goes very red.'

GB1 scratched her face slightly. 'But they are general groups, how do you know what type of meat fish etcetera is causing the problem?'

'Well that should come to light in the BER machine test that Dr Malinowski will do after I have finished.' Cheng did the tests, and no problems were observed.

Malinowski set up the BER machine and headed the black torch to GB1. 'If you would like to grab that device, I will then keep prodding your other hand to go through some 100 categories of food and drinks.'

'That sounds interesting, I look forward to the conclusion of this one, good or bad,' said GB1.

Malinowski started the test and for fifteen minutes no red light was observed. And then seven food items in a row were observed. Malinowski paused the machine and turned to the patient and asked her to relax. 'So we have a few problem fruits. They are blackcurrant, melon, peaches, apple, bananas, pear, and orange.'

GB1 looked puzzled. 'I am not aware of any problems with those fruit items, strange, most strange.' Malinowski resumed and carried on quickly. A bit of time went by.

'Lobster and crab, no good.' GB1 blinked but made no comment.

'You have a deficiency in vitamin D and zinc.'

GB1 thanked Malinowski and Cheng as she left the treatment room.

The telephone rang and Cheng answered. 'Okay thanks, Jenny.' Cheng turned to Malinowski. 'Our last patient, TW1, cannot make it today. She has a stomach pain and is resting in her room.'

CHAPTER 19

DAY NINETEEN
ALCOHOL AND NON-ALCOHOL TESTS

Dr Audrey Tan and Nurse Asterina Cheng were busy preparing the bottle and thimbles for the drinks test. The large table in the treatment room was covered with all manner of items. Tan picked up a clipboard and looked at the schedule. 'So we will be having patients in pairs,' she said.

'I suppose each test will be quite spaced out,' inquired Cheng.

'Yes, we will need five minutes between each category. There are five alcoholic drinks, namely beer, cider, vodka, gin, and whiskey. There are also five soft drinks categories – orange, lemon, grapefruit, passion fruit, and durian. So ten drinks for the patients spaced five minutes in between,' replied Tan.

Cheng looked at the table, she walked all the way round to see if it was ready. 'Okay I'll have a look to see if our first two patients are in the waiting area.' TW1 and SG1 were in the waiting area and Cheng called to them, 'Come this way please.' They entered the treatment room and were shown to the area where two comfortable chairs were placed together. Tan walked over to their area and smiled widely. 'Okay so today we are testing some drinks, both alcoholic and non-alcoholic, to see if there are any reactions to them. You will only be required to drink a thimble of each category. There will be a ten-minute resting period between each drink to allow time for regular reactions.'

TW1 looked at SG1 and then Tan. 'Sounds like fun.'

Tan put her head to one side. 'Maybe, we'll see.'

SG1 commented, 'It's a pity it's only a thimble full.'

Tan laughed, 'Ah well we don't want anyone getting drunk, do we? One other thing to tell you, there is some small pieces of bread to eat between each drink if you so please, it's entirely optional. We will alternate between an alcoholic drink and a non-alcoholic drink. The first one is beer so if I just set them for you.' Tan turned around and walked to the table, poured some beer from a prepared bottle, and filled two thimbles, placed them on a tray, and returned to the two patients. 'There we go, just a well-known beer for you to drink.' The two patients took the thimbles and drank simultaneously.

SG1 smiled and said, 'Lovely.' TW1 stared a coughing fit that went on for a while. Tan handed TW1 a tissue.

'Looks like you may be allergic to beer then.' TW1 blew her nose in to a tissue.

'How strange, I don't normally drink beer but in the past that did not happen if I had a beer, weird.'

Five minutes passed and the next drink, which was orange juice, had no adverse reaction. Cider, lemon, and vodka were the same. When the two patients had drunk their grapefruit TW1 again had a reaction. She coughed badly, just like after drinking the beer. Cheng shouted from the computer. 'I'll note it on the records.' TW1 shook her head and SG1 patted her on the back. The remaining drinks were fine for both patients.

SG2 and SG4 were the next pair of patients to be tested. SG2 told SG4 that she rarely drunk alcohol and preferred tea and coffee. SG4 said she liked wine but little else.

Cheng filled two thimbles with beer and placed them on a tray and held the tray in front of the two patients. SG2 drank hers quicker than SG4. 'Nice,' she remarked.

SG4 drank hers and remarked, 'Not that great. Never really took to beer, whatever the variety.' Cheng carried the thimbles to the dishwasher and returned to sit near the patients.

'So now a five-minute gap period just see if there are any reactions to the beer,' Cheng said, sitting down and folding her arms. SG4 looked at SG2 then Cheng.

'I don't know how guys can consume large quantities of beer,' SG2 smiled. 'I think it depends on the beer. There are so many types of beer these days. We sampled lager beer but there are more interesting drinks.'

'I suppose so,' said SG4.

The remaining tests went quite well but SG4 complained she felt a little dizzy after the vodka and had a slight coughing fit after the whiskey. SG2 was fine until the vest last item – the durian. This drink made her feel a little nauseous. 'Cannot stand the smell of durian,' she shrieked. Cheng agreed.

'No one likes the smell of durian.'

Even hotels in Singapore will not let the tourists take the durian fruit in to the rooms.

SG5 and ML2 arrived in good spirits and waited impatiently for testing to start. SG5 looked at ML2. 'This will be interesting because I only normally drink beer. Never really been into alcohol.'

ML2 laughed, 'I'm afraid I like to drink quite a lot with my friends. They lead me astray sometimes.'

SG5 nodded his head. 'Well, you are only young once.'

The first two drinks were fine for both the patients and then on test three SG5 complained of feeling a bit dizzy.

Cheng noted the response and carried on. The next drink was lemon. This time ML2 had a slight pain in the stomach. 'That's weird,' she said, holding her stomach. 'Not really had a problem with soft drinks before. I'm sure there's some acidity in lemon.' The remaining tests were completed, and the only problem was SG5 had a little reaction to gin.

'It's the same dizzy as it was a while back with the cider,' he said, shaking his head from side to side.

Meanwhile, Professor Lee was typing on his computer and heard a gentle knock at the door. 'Come in,' he said loudly. In walked Tasmin Chow, the wife of HK1. 'Have a seat. I'll be with you in a moment,' said Lee, turning back to his computer.

'Thanks,' said Chow, sitting on the chair by Lee's desk. A minute or two passed and Lee finished typing with a flourish and a firm press on the final words on the keyboard. 'Tasmin, how are you?' he inquired. Chow brushed her hair back from her eye.

'I have just seen Tony in the morgue and said goodbye to him.' Lee didn't know what to say so said nothing. Chow looked sad and stuttered to continue. 'Er, I presume there is only a small suitcase of Tony's stuff to take away?'

Lee picked up the phone on his desk and smiled at Chow. 'I'll get it collected now from the room.' Lee dialled the receptionist who took a while to answer. 'Jenny, can you get someone to collect HK1's suitcase from the room please? Thanks.' Lee put the phone down and pushed the phone away slightly.

Lee looked at Chow. 'Can I get you a drink?'

'I'm fine,' said Chow. Lee shuffled some papers and then cleared his throat.

'There'll be a postmortem on your husband to find out as

much as possible.'

Chow smiled, 'I would like to know what caused Tony to have such a dramatic heart attack. We know Tony was pushing himself to exhaustion with gambling, drinking, and smoking.'

'Have you enjoyed your stay in Singapore?' Lee asked.

'Yes,' she replied emphatically. 'I have met up with a few people I know. Everywhere clean, unlike Hong Kong.'

'How about our food?' asked Lee.

'Well, it's about the same standard as Hong Kong. I think we may have dim sum restaurants, but you have a great variety.'

There was a knock at the door and a hospital porter carried a suitcase into Lee's office. 'There we go,' he said.

'Do you want to check the contents? I can leave you for a few minutes as I need the toilet,' offered Lee. Chow nodded.

'Okay, thanks a lot, Benjamin.'

Meanwhile, back in the treatment room, the final two patients had arrived for drinks testing. ML1 and GB1 whispered together. Tan joined them and went through the procedure for the forthcoming tests. GB1 stared at Tan. 'How will we know if we have a problem with a drink?'

Tan smiled. 'You will mainly cough or feel dizzy or maybe get a stomach-ache.'

ML1 chipped in, 'How accurate are these kinds of tests?'

Tan looked serious. 'Don't know. But we are using so many tests on this experiment we overlap in some areas and hope to get a conclusion from that.' Testing started well from both patients but then ML1 had a problem with cider. He held his stomach for a moment. 'Got a problem?' asked Tan.

ML1 looked at the floor and then up at Tan. 'It doesn't

feel right. It's like my stomach is on a whirl. Going around and around.'

'Interesting,' said Tan, and then further commenting, 'Have you drunk cider before?'

'No, I don't recall trying it. We have it in my restaurant but it's not that popular. I think some of the cans even go past their sell-by date and have to be poured down the sink!' explained ML1.

A few more tests went well and then GB1 seemed to get a reaction to grapefruit. A sneezing fit followed as soon as she had drunk the sample. Tan asked, 'What did it taste like?'

GB1 thought for a moment. 'I suppose I found it a bit too sharp for my liking.'

CHAPTER 20

DAY TWENTY

THE RETURN OF THE BAD MAN

Dr Wong walked into the laboratory and then into Dr Malinowski's office. 'Alright?' he asked politely.

'I'm okay, I think,' replied Malinowski. Wong sat down next to his colleague. 'I was thinking about the MK888 roll out times.' Malinowski looked at her PC, then at Wong. 'Obviously a lot depends on our findings here in our experiment and any others taking place.'

'Do you know of any other trial runs overseas?' he enquired.

'I believe a similar testing is planned in Brazil at the end of the year,' Malinowski replied.

'Why Brazil?' asked Wong.

'I don't know. In that country they have a lot of cigarette smokers so one would assume that there are a large number of people with a coughing problem.'

Professor Lee looked at his computer at the schedule for the weeks ahead. He had one operation pencilled in for a patient with a damaged ear. The patient had tried to remove wax from his ear with a pen top and in the process damaged the ear drum. Lee heard the door open and quickly swivelled around in his chair. Standing in the doorway was SG3. The young art student had returned. He had returned with a gun in his hand and an angry expression on his face.

Lee stared at him and then asked, 'Where have you been?' SG3 closed the door behind him and walked towards Lee and sat down. Lee felt a little sweat on his forehead and fear was running through his mind. SG3 rested the gun on his right thigh.

'I have been unwell since the Electric Shock Test.'

Lee looked concerned and asked, 'Why did you discharge yourself?'

SG3 sighed. 'I couldn't stand it here. My mind has gone crazy, and I cannot eat or sleep. I feel depressed. It's just awful.' Lee looked at his patient's face and didn't care for the menacing look. Lee's gaze switched to the gun and then back to SG3.

He said nervously, 'Where did you get that gun, you cannot easily buy a gun in Singapore?' SG3 stared at Lee intensely. He sneezed twice and then answered the doctor.

'I got the gun in Malaysia; I know the right people.' By now Lee didn't know what to do or what to say. He was feeling in great danger. He was alone in his office with an angry patient who appeared to have serious mental health issues.

Lee was becoming frustrated and frightened. He shook his head from left to right. 'Please put the gun down on the table and we'll work out how you can be helped.'

SG3 snapped, 'You can't help me.'

Lee raised his voice. 'Look I've got work to do, I'm a busy man.' SG3 said nothing but stared at Lee and tightened the grip on the gun that he was still holding. Lee stood up and shouted. 'I think you should leave, NOW!'

SG3 got up and pointed the gun at Lee and shouted, 'I'm not going anywhere until I have shot you and Doctor Tan.' Very quickly Lee dived at SG3 and grabbed at the arm that was holding the gun with both hands. They fell to the floor and struggled together. Bang! The gun went off, firing a bullet into the chandelier on the ceiling and hitting two bulbs. Glass shattered on to the floor. They continued rolling around the floor. Lee tried to grab the gun from SG3 as he held on to it tightly. Bang! Another shot was fired. And then another bang! Both bullets hit the computer on Lee's desk. A loud pop was heard followed by sparks for several seconds and then another loud bang! The loud noise had caused Lee to drop the gun and it slipped from his hand to the wooden floor, spinning away in the process. SG3 stood up and dived on to the floor, hoping to regain the weapon. Just as he put his hand on the gun, Lee had given his hand an all-mighty kick. The gun went spinning under the desk and SG3 screamed in pain. He cried out and held his injured hand with his other hand. Lee stared at him without moving. SG3 breathed heavily and then suddenly left the office, still groaning in pain.

Lee struggled to his desk and sat down in shock. He grabbed a tissue from his desk and wiped his forehead which was now soaked in sweat. The computer was still smoking from the damage. Lee nervously knelt under the desk and turned the electric off. He got back to his chair and sat down. He poured himself a glass of water and with a shaking hand drank it all in one go. Lee struggled to stop trembling but gave himself five minutes and then picked up the phone. 'Police, could I have a police visit? Something terrible has happened. It's Professor Lee from Singapore ENT Hospital. I've just been threatened with a gun. From one of my patients. No, the culprit has fled my office. Cairnhill Circle. Thank you so much.' Lee slammed the phone down and sighed. He poured himself another glass of water.

Lee placed his head in his hands and sat motionless for what seemed a lifetime. The phone rang. Jenny on reception told Lee the police officers had arrived. Quickly the policeman arrived at Lee's office. They sat down and looked at the damaged computer and the broken glass on the floor. Lee started to tell the officers what had happened. 'One of my patients, a young Singaporean male, had been taking part in a new drug experiment here at this hospital. One of the tests we carried out on this fellow was an Electric Shock Test. To cut a long story short it had some adverse effects where the patient, SG3, suffered terrible nightmares, loss of appetite, sleeplessness. He discharged himself from the hospital three days ago without telling anyone. So, he returned today and burst into my office with a gun. Threatened to shoot me and said he wanted to shoot Doctor Tan, who set up the electric shock test.'

The two police officers looked at each other and then the one who was writing the notes said, 'What time was this?'

'Approximately three o' clock this afternoon,' replied Lee. 'SG3 sat in my office with the gun in his hand and we had a brief discussion and then he said he wanted to shoot me. I stood up and he stood up. Then I lunged towards him to try and get the gun. We both fell to the floor and wrestled for the gun.'

The other officer said, 'Where is the gun now?' Lee scratched his head, reflecting events.

'It rolled under my desk I think.' The officer looked under the desk.

'I can see it.' He pulled out a cloth and plastic bag from the case he was carrying and placed it neatly in the bag.

'So what happened next?'

Lee put his head to one side. 'We struggled for the gun for a while and then I think three shots were fired. The first hit the chandelier, as you can see it has lost two bulbs. Then a second and third bullet hit my computer. Shortly after the gunfire the gun slipped from SG3's hand and spun on the floor away from us. SG3 got to his feet to try and get the gun. I also arose from the floor quickly and managed to kick his hand hard just as he was about to grab it. The gun went flying under my desk and SG3 gasped in pain, holding his hand as he got up. After he got his composure back, he just fled my office.'

'What time was this?' asked the officer taking notes. Lee looked at his watch and then spoke.

'Roughly half an hour ago.'

The officer noted Lee's words and then asked, 'Do you have a photo and personal details of the guy in question? Address, phone number?' Lee looked at his now useless computer and smiled.

'I'll have to get a colleague to give you that detail.'

'Can you do it now and we can keep a look out at all the Singapore exit areas like airport, world trade centre, Johor Causeway at Woodlands, the causeway crossing at Tuas, etc.'

'Right, no problem,' said Lee, picking up the phone and dialling quickly. 'Fu, Benjamin here. I have been threatened today by SG3… Yes he came back with a gun and threatened me, anyway I'll fill you in later, but I am with the police now in my office, my computer got shot at and I am unable to use it. The police require details urgently about SG3. Photo, description, phone number etc. You'll find it all in the patient's records. I'll just pass you over to the officer and he can give you the email address of where to send the info, hold on please.' Lee gave the phone to the officer who then gave

Fu the email address.

The officers left Lee to his office and shambles of the incident. He packed some papers in his briefcase and left the office and walked to reception. He waited for Jenny to come off the phone and then told her he was taking the rest of the day off because of the incident.

Cleaners arrived in Lee's office and removed the debris and broken glass from the floor. Just as they were finishing, two guys turned up from IT with new computer terminal after taking a photo of the damaged old monitor. After a few minutes setting up, they sprayed the new computer and removed dust from the keyboard.

Dr Fu Su Wong picked up the phone and it was a call from the police confirming they had received an email from him with all the details they had requested. The policeman told Wong they had tried calling the patient's mobile but got no answer. All Singapore exit points were alerted to look for any sighting of SG3. His home address would be paid a visit and, if unsuccessful, relatives would be contacted.

CHAPTER 21

DAY TWENTY-ONE
VISITING HOME

GB1 sat in reception reading a magazine while waiting for Dr Tan to meet her. GB1 had invited Tan to her home for lunch. After five minutes Tan arrived. 'Shall we go?' she smiled. GB1 stood up and walked to the door leading out onto the street and held it open for Tan.

'Thank you,' Tan said gratefully. They walked slowly along Cairnhill Circle, admiring the high-rise luxury condos. 'Quite tall, aren't they?' commented Tan. '

Yes, but I don't like condos. I am so lucky to live in a house,' said GB1.

In very little time they arrived at the start of Emerald Hill. GB1 pointed to her house. 'The red and white one is my house.' Tan looked gobsmacked.

'So large, do you know when it was built?'

GB1 thought for a moment and then replied. 'I believe it was in the nineteen twenties. They were originally houses inhabited by people who ran small businesses from their properties.'

They arrived at the property and GB1 opened the door and gestured for her guest to enter. Tan smiled and entered the large hall which had mahogany-panelled walls. GB1 closed the door behind her. 'I'll just give you a tour on the house before we have lunch.'

'Lovely,' said Tan, excited.

GB1 showed her guest every room and they eventually found their way to the kitchen/diner. 'It's a fantastic house, how did you collect so many ancient relics?' said Tan.

'Well my father had been in the antiques business and travelled extensively in Asia. Also, my husband's grandmother owned the house before and a lot of her stuff is still here. One of my favourite purchases is the dark wooden chest at the top of the stairs. I bought that in Chang Mai, Thailand, a few years ago.'

'Yes, the work in that piece is stunning. How many elephants in the carvings in total?' asked Tan.

'I really don't know,' answered GB1. 'Maybe one day I'll count them.'

They sat at the large kitchen table and GB1 asked her guest if she would like a drink. 'A Chinese tea would be welcome,' replied Tan. GB1 walked over to the cupboard and got some tea and made two drinks.

Carrying them to the table she said, 'We are having some seafood delivered for our lunch.'

'Where from?' Tan inquired.

'It's coming from Ponggol seafood restaurant in Punggol Point. Do you know it?'

'Cannot say I do,' replied Tan.

Just as they were enjoying the Chinese tea the doorbell rang loudly. 'Are here we are, that'll be our lunch delivery.' GB1 opened the door, took the two bags of food, and thanked the delivery man. GB1 placed the bags of food on the table and removed each little box and placed them neatly in pairs. She went to the cutlery drawer in the kitchen and returned with a selection of forks and spoons. 'Right, let's see what we have here,' she said. One by one all the food was revealed. GB1 pointed to each dish and then described them. 'Obviously egg fried rice, sweet and sour pork, chilli crab, mee goreng, prawns in butter, fried chicken with shrimp paste, and Singapore noodles. Eight items.'

'Wow, we'll never eat all this,' shrieked Tan.

'Don't worry, my husband will have some this evening for his evening meal. He's a big eater.' They piled food on to their plates and happily munched away. 'Would you like more Chinese tea?' asked GB1.

'Yes, I will, please,' replied Tan. GB1 made a large pot and returned. The ladies continued eating.

'Is it all good?' asked GB1.

'All very nice,' replied Tan. 'What do you make of HK1?'

'I didn't really get to know him that well. It seems he had a very strange lifestyle. Obviously, being a professional gambler there is no happy medium. They are either on cloud nine if they are winning or down in the dumps when they are losing money. I passed him once in the hall and he stank of alcohol.'

The two of them ate until the point of no return. 'Well stuffed,' sighed Tan.

'Me too,' added GB1. GB1 poured more Chinese tea for the both of them.

Tan looked seriously at GB1. 'Did you hear that trouble yesterday with SG3?'

GB1 looked worried. 'No, what trouble was that?' Tan shook her head from side to side.

'What happened was he returned to the hospital yesterday afternoon and marched into Professor Lee's office with a gun and threatened him.'

'Oh my god,' said GB1 in disbelief.

'Apparently there was a struggle when Lee tried to get the gun off him and a shot was fired and hit the ceiling light, another bullet hit the computer on Lee's desk. It seems the Electric Shock Test had some serious side effects, and he was not felt the same since. His plan was to shoot the Professor and me too, if he had found me.'

'Phew, what can you say? I wonder if he had been taking any illegal substances,' said GB1.

'Well Dr Wong emailed the police a photo and various personal details and they are on the lookout for him,' said Tan.

GB1 tidied up the table and put the dirty plates in the dishwasher and turned it on. 'Where do live, Audrey?'

'I am in ECP, not far from the airport. Four of us in the condo. My husband, me, and two daughters,' replied Tan. 'We have a view of the ships coming in.' Tan looked at her watch. 'I better be getting back, thanks for a nice lunch, and the house tour.'

'You are welcome,' said GB1. They exchanged goodbyes and Tan made her way back to the hospital.

CHAPTER 22

DAY TWENTY-TWO
WEEK 3 REVIEW

Professor Lee stormed in the meeting room and apologised for arriving ten minutes late. All patients were present apart from the missing SG3. The medical team was all present for the meeting.

Lee looked around the room at everyone and then got the meeting started. 'Welcome everyone, we are on day twenty-two of our MK888 experiment. Today we are having our week three review of events to date. I don't know how many of you are aware, but two days ago our missing patient SG3 returned to the hospital. But he didn't come back to re-join the experiment! He came back with a gun and marched into my office and threatened to shoot me! We had words, I tried to grab the gun from him, and we struggled on the floor before the gun actually went off. A bullet hit the light in my office, and a further two bullets hit my computer, producing a cloud of smoke. The gun slid on the floor and we both tried to grab it. SG3 dived on the floor and just when he was about to pick up the gun, I kicked his hand very hard and the gun connected as well, spinning under my desk. SG3 got to his feet, holding his injured hand with the other hand, gasping in pain. After a few minutes he just left my office. When I got my composure back, I called the police. They arrived soon after, taking a statement from me of the events. When they left, I asked Dr Wong to email the police a photo and other personal data to help them look for the young man.' Lee cleared his throat.

'So, how has everyone been doing? As usual I will go around the table and ask for feedback on what individuals have experienced. SG1 could you tell us your thoughts on the last week?'

SG1 smiled and looked around the table. 'I am pleased to report that I have coughed less than normal in the past week. When I say less than normal, I mean before this MK888 experiment started. There does not appear to be any side effects from the medication.'

Lee nodded. 'Good, how about SG2 then?'

SG2 coughed twice. 'Excuse me, yes, this week I found out I have a dairy intolerance. Not surprised, I had thought it for a while. My coughing is the same as the previous weeks, and the same prior to this experiment. I have no side effects to report from the MK888 tablets so far.' Lee thanked SG2 and then looked around the table.

'SG4, how has your week been?'

SG4 sneezed loudly. 'Excuse me, I enjoyed the week, good food intolerance testing, including the BER machine. Not too much negative on my side. But I have had a week of coughing more than normal, combined with a sore throat and stomach pain.'

Lee sat up higher in his chair. 'Is the stomach pain soon after taking the MK888 tablets?'

'Usually yes,' replied SG4.

Lee thought for a moment. 'It might be advisable to adjust the medication a little.' Lee looked at Doctor Wong who was sitting next to him. 'Could you meet up with SG4 tomorrow and go through the medication?'

'Okay I'll do that,' Wong turned to look at SG4 down the other end of the table. 'Say four in the afternoon tomorrow,' he said.

SG4 replied gratefully, 'Fine, see you then.'

Lee looked around the table and found SG5. 'SG5, how was your week three?'

'I have had a bit better week. I had been sleeping poorly and the first sleeping tablets prescribed didn't seem to help. In the last seven days I have been on another tablet and it helped me to sleep better. I can also report a bit of reduction in my coughing.'

Lee smiled. 'No side effects of the MK888 tablets?'

'No it's only been the poor sleeping in the first two weeks of the experiment,' answered SG5.

Lee looked at his paperwork and then looked around the table. 'ML1, how is your week three?'

ML1 sighed. 'Not great. The stomach-ache I had in week one has returned in week three. In week two it didn't happen so a bit concerned with it.' Lee made a note and then looked at ML1.

'I'll prescribe something to help stop the stomach pain.' ML1 nodded.

'Thanks for the help.'

ML2 was the next to report. 'I have coughed less this week than the two previous two. As with regards to side effects, I don't recall anything to report. When I was on the BER machine test it was confirmed what I believed about nuts. I have a problem with them so will avoid that kind of snack in the foreseeable future.'

GB1 coughed three times before giving her account of the

week. 'Yes, so, as you can see, I'm still coughing. I can report the headaches have reduced compared to week two. But I have a new problem this week. That problem is stomach-ache. It has been unpleasant at times. Cannot pin down to anything in particular. The medication or the food I've had, perhaps.' Lee wrote some notes.

'Okay, I'll prescribe you something for the stomach-ache.'

TW1 was the last to give account of the week. 'My stomach-ache has gone this week and my coughing is not quite so bad. Other than that, nothing to report.'

On the north side of Singapore, in an area called Yishun, the two policemen in charge of looking for the missing patient SG3 sat in a patrol car parked near a shopping centre. They watched people and traffic go by. Policeman 1 looked at Policeman 2 and asked if he would like a coffee. He agreed that was a good idea. Policeman 1 got out of the car and walked into a coffee shop close by. He returned with coffees and custard buns. Policeman 2 took the coffee and bun from his colleague.

'Thanks, that is just what the stomach ordered.' They munched away happily on their tarts and slurped the coffee periodically.

Policeman 2 took the empty cups and bags, got out of the car, and discarded them in a bin. He returned to the car and was about to get in when, from the corner of his eye, he thought he saw the missing patient. 'Sarge, I think I just spotted our missing man go in a shop over there.' Policeman 1 got out of the car and locked it. He got on his walkie talkie.

'I'd like to report a sighting of SG3 in Yishun Avenue 2, now in pursuit of him together with a colleague. Check, maybe we can count on assistance from another officer and constable parked in Yishun Park area, over.'

A crackling sounding voice replied, 'Will contact the other officers in Yishun Avenue 1 and inform them of the situation. Over and out.'

'Thanks,' said Policeman 1. He re-fixed his walkie talkie to his trouser top. 'Okay let's try and arrest him.'

Policeman 2 said, 'I think he went into the shop next to Seven Eleven just up there.' The two policemen walked quickly and, at the point they were a hundred yards away from the shop in question, SG3 walked out and looked to face them. SG3 quickly turned and ran in the opposite direction. The policemen ran quickly in pursuit but after turning a corner they had lost him.

The sergeant got out his walkie talkie. 'It's PC50 here, myself and PC51 were in pursuit of the villain in Yishun Avenue 2 but lost sight of him. Can you message the other police in the area to keep a look out? The suspect has black hair with ginger and blue streaks. He is wearing blue jeans, sneakers, and a bright yellow and blue T-shirt. The suspect is around five-feet-seven and weighing fifty kilos … Thanks, over and out.

CHAPTER 23

DAY TWENTY-THREE
LEGAL THREAT

Professor Lee sat in his office typing notes on the computer. The telephone rang. Lee answered. 'Jasmin, how are you? … I know nothing about a missing pen belonging to Tony. Don't worry I'll make enquiries and have the room searched from top to bottom … You are joking! Oh come on, Jasmin, Tony only had two weeks exposure to MK888. It couldn't possibly be a contributory factor to his death.' Lee slapped his right fist on his desk in anger. 'Well if you want to pursue that route it's up to you but I think you'll have no chance … Okay, bye Jasmin.' Lee thumped his desk hard with his fist and screamed, 'Fucking bitch.'

Lee picked up the phone and called the hospital's lawyers. 'Can I speak to Charles Goh please? … Charles, how are you? Okay, I'm in the middle of an experiment testing a new drug, for coughs … Yes going well, I think. Having said that, one patient has had a heart attack and sadly died on us. A Hong Kong gentleman died on day fourteen of the experiment. Nothing to do with MK888. But I just had a call from his wife to say if there is anything amiss in the toxicology report she may sue the hospital … That's why I am ringing you to ask where we might stand legally with such a claim against us … Okay you'll drop by this afternoon? That's great. See you later, Charles. Thanks.' Lee smiled to himself.

Dr Wong knocked on the door of SG4 and heard a voice offering admission. They exchanged hellos. Wong asked, 'Could we do your medical review earlier? We did say four this afternoon but I've had something crop up and need to reschedule a few things.'

'Fine, I have nothing planned for today so just say when is good,' replied SG4.

Wong looked at his watch. 'Could you come to my office in twenty minutes?'

'See you then,' smiled SG4.

SG4 knocked on Wong's door and entered. 'Have a seat,' said Wong while typing on his computer. SG4 sat down and a few minutes passed then Wong finished typing and turned to face to his patient. 'How's it going then?' Wong asked.

'So so, as I said yesterday in the weekly review, I am suffering like some of the others with stomach pain. Also, I have an increase in coughing plus a sore throat,' replied SG4.

Wong turned to look at his computer and started typing. 'I'll give you some good cough mixture for the cough and some tablets to reduce acid in the stomach. We are not sure but Dr Malinowski and I think MK888 produces acid in the stomach.' Wong printed off a schedule of medication and gave it to the patient. 'Give that to pharmacy and we'll see if that helps. When is your cancer treatment starting?' SG4 raised her eyebrows before speaking.

'I don't know. In a few weeks I have the radiotherapy pre-treatment measuring procedure done.'

'Yeah that'll be a CT scan to get a precise measuring of the cancer area,' added Wong.

Charles Goh met Professor Lee in reception and they walked to Lee's office. After sitting down, Lee asked Goh if he would like a drink. Goh declined the offer. Lee walked to his filing cabinet and pulled out a folder, he returned to his chair and slumped down. 'Right, Charles, here is the patient consent form.'

Goh rolled his eyes. 'You see, this is an experiment with an unknown outcome. The patient agreed to participate in this experiment and agreed to the risks involved, and as long as all medical guidelines are met, I don't see a problem. I'll just take a copy back to the office and run it past a colleague.'

'Yes, that's fine,' said Lee. 'The woman is neurotic, Jasmin Chow that is. You know, she even asked for a fifty per cent return of the experiment fee?'

Goh looked at the paperwork again and then smiled at Lee. 'So, all patients were to be paid fifty thousand Singapore dollars on completing the course?'

'That's right,' confirmed Lee. 'But that means completing the course and returning after three months for further tests and for keeping a record of medical conditions in the time between.'

'Interesting,' nodded Goh. 'So, Mrs Chow is looking for a payment of twenty-five thousand dollars?'

Lee gritted his teeth. 'She can fuck off as far as I am concerned.'

Goh asked, 'Can I keep the consent form?'

'Yes that's one of many in my cabinet,' confirmed Lee. Goh put the form in his briefcase.

'What's next after this MK888 is finished?' Goh put his head to one side.

'I have a number of lectures planned. Both in Singapore and overseas. A new ENT hospital is opening in Taipei, Taiwan, and I have been asked to help with some of the groundwork.'

Goh nodded. 'That could be fun.'

'Oh, it will be fun. It's always fun in Taiwan,' concluded Lee.

CHAPTER 24

DAY TWENTY-FOUR
UNPAID BAR BILL

Dr Wong sat in his office reading a medical magazine. His mobile phone vibrated and then started ringing. He answered quickly. 'Dr Wong here … Really? You better come in and see me, Harry. You can come now or four-thirty this afternoon? … Okay I'll see you in a bit.' Twenty minutes went by and Harry Choo, a local bar owner, was sitting in Wong's office.

Wong smiled at Harry. 'So how have you been, Harry? I've not seen you for a long time.'

'Business is quite good. Lots of tourists as well as locals.'

'Good. You said on the phone that a patient from here owes you money for drinks.'

'Yes, a honkey came in my bar on a number of occasions, but he didn't always pay for the drinks he had. He told me he was a patient at this hospital and taking part in an interesting medical experiment,' explained Harry, adjusting his seat.

'So you are saying your bar is owed money by one of our patients. I don't think I can help because the patient in question is dead. He suffered a heart attack and died around 11 days ago.' Harry Choo shook his head from side to side in disbelief. Wong continued. 'I'm surprised you gave credit to someone you don't know. Why no credit card payment?'

Harry replied, 'Well, the first two visits he paid by credit card, no problem. But then there were another three visits where he said he forgot his card and he would settle up on the next visit.'

'I see,' said Wong.

Harry felt in his trouser pocket and produced a bar receipt and gave it to Wong. Wong looked closely at the detail. 'Our patients are not supposed to drink while they are on medication. Five hundred and twelve dollars for whiskeys. What was he drinking?'

'Blend 88 is a vintage whiskey. Very popular with honkers.' Wong looked again and smiled widely.

'It cannot be.'

'What's that?' Harry asked.

'You are not still running a bar with girls? Hostess fee, one thousand dollars. Harry, really!'

Harry looked serious. 'Well, I have an expensive wife, I need the money coming in.' Wong shook his head in disgust.

'One thousand dollars for a hostess. So, all together you are owed one thousand five hundred and twelve dollars.'

'Yes, that's right,' confirmed Harry. Wong looked away and then back to Harry.

'I'll speak with Professor Lee but I'm not hopeful that we can reimburse you for the bar bill incurred by HK1. His wife is due the pro-rata fee for the time that he participated in the experiment. We might be able to take it off that, I don't know.'

'If you could try, I'd appreciate it,' pleaded Harry.

Wong smiled at Harry. 'How's your blood pressure?'

'Dunno,' replied Harry.

'Roll up your sleeve and I'll take it,' said Wong. Harry rolled up his shirt sleeve and Wong immediately fitted the wrap-round cloth on to the arm. He pressed the button on the box and the whirring sound started. Wong stared at the box and waited for the BP machine to give its reading. '165 over 85. Harry, that's not good,' he said in a serious tone.

Harry didn't seem too bothered. 'Well I like a drink and a few burgers, so what!'

Wong asked, 'Can you give up alcohol for a few months?' Harry slumped back in his chair.

'Nah, I love a drink too much.'

'It's up to you, Harry, but you are in danger of heart trouble or even a stroke. I suggest, if you are unable to give up the booze, cut it down by half and take regular exercise.'

Harry sighed. 'Okay I'll take your advice.'

Wong quickly followed up, 'I do not mean go to the gym every day or run five miles once a week. Do small things regularly. Go for walks. Go cycling or swimming. Cut back on the junk food and the heavy drinking. This all helps to reduce the high blood pressure.'

Harry thought for a moment. 'I previously was swimming quite a lot. I liked it before.'

Wong briefly looked at his computer and then back to Harry. 'Yes, so I'll see what I can do for you on the unpaid bill and let you know.'

'Thanks Fu,' said Harry, standing up to leave. 'I'll see myself out. Good luck with the MK888 experiment.'

On the other side of the hospital, ML1 was playing a game on his computer in his room. There was a knock at the door and a young man entered. 'Hi, IT, I need to update your software.' ML1 quickly ended his computer game.

'Be my guest,' he said, getting up from his chair and walking over to the bed to sit down.

Meanwhile, in the library, SG5 slipped on the floor and fell on his bad hip. 'Oh shit,' he shrieked. Nobody else was present in the library and he sat on the floor for a few minutes. A nurse walked by the library door and notice SG5 in distress. She walked in quickly. 'What happened, sir?'

SG5 spoke, a little disorientated, 'I don't know, I just seemed to fall and could not save myself.'

The nurse put her arm around him. 'I'll take you down to X-ray, just to be on the safe side.'

'Thanks,' said SG5, limping his way to the X-ray department.

CHAPTER 25

DAY TWENTY-FIVE
SMOKE CHAMBER TEST

Cheng and Malinowski sorted the various boxes into piles. Cigarette, barbecue, and food-related were the three types chosen for the smoke test. Cheng took a damp cloth into the smoke chamber and wiped the seat with it. Malinowski shouted to Cheng, 'Eight patients taking three tests means we need twenty-four smoke cannisters, right?'

Cheng walked out of the smoke chamber. 'Correct.' Malinowski counted the three piles.

'I only count twenty-three canisters.'

Cheng pointed to the chest in the corner. 'There's one more on the desk, it should be cigarette smoke and that pile looks slightly less than the other two.' Malinowski retrieved it and placed the box on the cigarette pile.

'All present and correct,' she smiled.

The door to the treatment room burst open and SG5 staggered in. 'Good morning to you,' he said. Cheng went to his aid.

'I heard about your fall yesterday. How are you feeling today?'

'So-so, I am a bit sore and I have a bad hip at the best of times but this incident has increased the pain there.'

Cheng guided him to a chair near the smoke chamber. 'Sit there,' she said. 'How did the X-ray go?'

SG5 slumped down in his chair. 'It was fine, no broken bones.'

Malinowski stood in front of SG5. 'Are you up to the Smoke Chamber Tests?' she asked.

SG5 smiled. 'Well, I cannot say I've been looking forward to it. But we will give it a try.'

Malinowski explained the tests to come. 'So, we will be putting you in that chamber behind you and carry out three tests. The chamber will be filled with a cigarette smoke substance for Test 1. Test 2 will be a barbecue smoke, and Test 3 will be a food-related smoke test.'

'That all sounds very interesting,' said SG5.

Cheng handed Malinowski the first smoke cartridge. Malinowski pointed to the chamber and SG5 entered quickly and closed the door. A minute later the cartridge had been loaded and things were ready to start. Malinowski looked at SG5 in the chamber and put her head up with her thumb raised to indicate the test was about to start. She pressed the 'on' button on the remote control. A whirring noise for about thirty seconds was followed by a burst of smoke. The smoke swirled around the chamber, aided by a fan. SG5 closed his eyes, and his face became slightly red. A second burst of smoke entered the chamber. SG5 put his hand to his mouth and started coughing. At first only mildly and then a loud continuous cough. Malinowski stopped the test immediately and open the door to the chamber quickly. As she helped the patient out of the chamber, he almost fell over and started a third round of coughing. SG5 sat in the treatment chair and wiped the sweat from his head. Cheng handed him a damp towel to cool him down.

Minutes went by and no words were spoken. Then SG5

looked at both medics. 'Phew, that was a choker. The smoke seemed to settle in my throat and then I could not stop coughing.'

'Are you feeling well enough to continue the tests?'

SG5 thought for a moment and then answered. 'Bring it on.' SG5 stood up and slowly entered the chamber for the second time, but immediately came back out. 'I feel unwell,' he gasped. Cheng prompted him to sit down, which he did slowly. 'No, I feel a bit faint. A bit fuzzy in the head.'

Malinowski stood close to him and said, 'I think we'll forget the other two tests. We don't want you to suffer unduly from these tests. Are you okay to walk back to your room?'

SG5 nodded. 'Yes, I think I'll be okay. I'll get some rest and take it easy for the rest of the day.' Malinowski smiled.

'Okay we'll leave it like that. We are sorry you had a bad reaction, but we learn a lot from these tests. Sometimes the side effects are not very nice, but there we are.'

SG5 got up and stretched his arms out wide and took a deep breath. 'I'll be off then, have a good day.' Cheng and Malinowski wished him goodbye.

Five minutes passed and the next patient arrived – SG2. Cheng welcomed SG2 to sit down while Malinowski sat at the computer. Cheng picked up a cartridge for the first test and waited for Malinowski to join her near the chamber. 'Thanks,' said Malinowski taking the cartridge. 'Now, SG2, we are going to do three tests in the chamber. You will be breathing in smoke. The first test is cigarette smoke, second is barbecue smoke, and the third is food related. If you feel really ill at any point, put your hand up and we'll stop the test straight away and let you out of the chamber.'

SG2 looked serious. 'Okay then, let's see what happens.'

Malinowski loaded the smoke cartridge into the side of the chamber.

'Please enter the chamber.' SG2 stood up, entered the chamber, closed the door, and sat down. Malinowski put her thumbs up and started the test. Smoke gradually filled the chamber. Two minutes passed and the patient did not cough at all. Malinowski opened the door and SG2 jumped out. Her eyes were streaming with tears but other than that she was okay.

'How was it?' asked Malinowski.

'Not too bad. Just my eyes are stinging a bit,' replied the patient. Malinowski seemed pleased and gave the patient time to relax before test two.

'Now the next one is a replica of barbecue smoke. It could be, shall I say, less unpleasant smell than the cigarette smoke. Are you ready for this next test?'

'Yes, ready,' said SG2, standing up and walking into the chamber. Malinowski loaded the cartridge in the machine and the humming started up. After thirty seconds the smoke started to appear. It had an uncanny likeness to a garden barbecue. Waves of smoke and then nearly nothing and then a build-up of thin and thick pieces of smoke swirled around the chamber. After two minutes Malinowski turned the machine off and released the patient from her ordeal. She looked red faced and tears were coming down from the eyes.

'How was the test?' Malinowski asked.

'Not too bad. I just feel a bit hot.'

Malinowski nodded. 'Will you do the last one?'

'Okay,' agreed SG2.

Cheng handed SG2 a glass of water. 'Drink that and have a ten-minute rest.'

The ten-minute break soon passed and SG2 was back in the chamber awaiting the third and final test. Malinowski gave the thumbs up and started the test. Thin smoke appeared and swirled around the chamber. SG2 watched the shapes with interest. After two minutes the test was finished. SG2 walked out unaffected, apart from another spell of watering eyes.

The next patient to be tested was SG1. When waiting for the test he had a small coughing fit and Cheng handed him a glass of water. 'Thank you very much,' he said, taking his water. Malinowski stood next to SG1 and went through the various tests briefly.

'Are you happy to take the three tests?'

'Yes, I am fit and ready for it.' Malinowski pointed to the chamber and the patient walked in and closed the door. Malinowski pressed the remote control, and nothing happened. 'Oh, what's wrong now?' she moaned. Cheng walked over to her aid.

'How about checking the batteries?' Malinowski took the back off the remote control and then took the four batteries out and replaced them back immediately. She pressed the on button and the normal whirring noise began. Cheng smiled widely. Within twenty seconds of the cigarette smoke, SG1 started coughing badly. Malinowski stopped the test and opened the door of the chamber. SG1 staggered out, still coughing.

'Don't like it,' he shrieked. 'Breathing in that shit, no good.' SG1 slumped into the chair by the chamber and closed his eyes.

Cheng asked, 'Are you going to be okay to continue?'

'Ah give me a minute or two to recover,' snapped SG1, opening and closing his eyes erratically.

Five minutes passed and SG1 stood up quickly. 'Okay let's do the second test,' he said loudly. Malinowski waited until the patient was settled on the chamber and relaxed. Malinowski started the test and the barbecue smoke swirled around SG1's head and he looked at it, fascinated by the movements. A minute passed by and SG1 started a continuous cough that was very loud. Malinowski stopped the test and helped him out of the chamber. 'I liked the smell but just like the first it hit the back of my throat and set me off coughing again,' he shrieked.

'Better off having another rest for five minutes,' suggested Cheng.

Five minutes went by and SG1 wiped his forehead and had a drink of water. 'Ready?' asked Malinowski.

'As I'll ever be,' snapped SG1. SG1 took his time getting back inside the chamber and, when seated, gave the thumbs up sign to indicate he was ready to start. The smoke swirled around and then stopped and shortly after came back in spurts. SG1 shook his head from side to side and then threw his arm up to indicate he wanted to stop the test. Cheng pushed the chamber door open and helped the patient out. SG1 looked red-faced and started another coughing fit just as he was sitting down in the chair. 'That was a load of crap,' he shrieked. 'An absolute load of shit. Cannot see the logic behind it.'

Cheng and Malinowski didn't know what to say to the patient, so they didn't say anything.

ML2 arrived and sat in the chair by the chamber. The room was full of her perfume. Malinowski looked at Cheng without speaking. Cheng knew that Malinowski disapproved of the smell of her perfume. ML2 wore tight jeans and a skimpy top and was shivering slightly. 'Can you turn the AC down a little? I'm feeling cold,' she said.

Malinowski replied, 'Okay, but you could have dressed more appropriate for the test.' ML2 gave Malinowski a dirty look of disapproval. Cheng walked over to the AC control box on the wall and turned up the temperature by a couple of degrees.

Test one went without a hitch. ML2 walked out of the chamber and, apart from a red face and slightly watering eyes, she seemed fine.

'How was it?'

ML2 replied. 'Not too bad. The smoke did smell just like cigarette smoke.'

Malinowski gave her a tissue for her eyes. 'We'll have a little rest and then go on to test number two which is the barbecue smoke test.'

ML2 returned to the chamber for the barbecue smoke test. Malinowski could not get the test going.

'I think we may have a dud cartridge for this one. Asterina, could you get another cartridge please?' Cheng took another cartridge from the pile and handed it to Malinowski. She swapped cartridges and started again. This time no problem. The smoke took longer than previous tests but appeared eventually. ML2 survived the test with no coughing and walked out. 'Not too bad,' she said.

Test three went well with no hiccups and the patient described the smell as rather like bacon or a roast meat dinner cooking.

ML1, the Malaysian restaurant owner, arrived with a smile. He was quite excited at the prospect of the tests, unlike some of the other patients. 'How have you been keeping?' asked Malinowski.

'I'm good. Longing to get back to work once this experiment is over.' Cheng handed him some water which he gratefully accepted as he sat down. Malinowski went through the tests briefly with him and he looked happy to endure them.

Test one started and went well but as soon as ML1 came out of the chamber he suffered quite a long and loud coughing fit. Malinowski helped him to the chair. 'It got me in the throat right at the end,' complained ML1.

'Never mind, have a break before the next test.'

Just as Malinowski was about to start the barbecue smoke test, ML1 put his hand up. Malinowski walked to the chamber and opened the door. 'What's up?' she asked.

'I just need to have a coughing fit,' explained ML1.

'Take your time,' advised Malinowski. Closing the door, ML1 coughed on and off for a minute. He blew his nose into a paper handkerchief, sat down, and then gave the thumbs up to continue. Malinowski put her thumb up to indicate the test was about to start. The test ran all of two minutes and ML1 emerged with a red face and a few tears rolling down his cheeks. 'Really smells of charcoal,' he said.

'Have a rest for a few minutes and we'll do the final one,' said Malinowski.

After five minutes had passed, ML1 was back in the chamber and eagerly waiting for test three to start. Malinowski pressed the on button on the remote. Nothing happened. She pressed again and again. 'Cheng, I think we got another faulty cartridge. Can you get me another food smoke cartridge?' snapped Malinowski. Cheng quickly got a fresh cartridge and placed it in the machine and threw the original one in a bin. Malinowski signalled to ML1 the test was about to start. It started and went full course. ML1 staggered out, red-faced, and sneezed then coughed once.

'Interesting,' he laughed. 'Smelt like my restaurant's kitchen on a busy night.'

'Well done,' said Cheng, handing him a drink of water.

TW1 arrived late for her testing, apologising profoundly. She sat down in the chair by the chamber. Cheng noticed she was somewhat flustered. 'Can I get you a water or a fruit juice perhaps?'

TW1 smiled. 'Okay, I'll have a fruit juice, thanks.'

'Pineapple or passion fruit?'

'I'll have the passion fruit, thank you.' Cheng went to the fridge and took out a small can and poured the drink in to a beaker and gave it to TW1. Malinowski explained the three tests and TW1 entered the chamber. The first two tests went without a hitch. The third test had a problem starting up but eventually started and finished within the required timescale.

GB1 was the next patient to arrive for testing. Malinowski explained the procedures to her. Cheng looked at GB1 and noticed her face was pale. 'How are you feeling today?' she asked.

'I've got a bit of a headache,' answered GB1.

Malinowski chipped in. 'Do you want to have these tests on another day?'

'I'd rather get them out of the way,' sighed GB1.

Test one with the cigarette smoke went well with no side effects. Test two was a little troublesome. GB1 came out of the chamber coughing and sneezing. 'That one has an uncanny likeness to a real barbecue,' she said.

Malinowski laughed. 'Yes, it's a mirror of the real thing.'

Test three for food smoke affected GB1 and had to be stopped halfway as she started coughing loudly and complained once of feeling dizzy.

The last patient, SG4, arrived in a good mood. She told Malinowski and Cheng that her cancer treatment program timetable would be ready in two or three weeks. SG4 entered the chamber for test one. Halfway through she raised her hand to indicate that she wanted the test to stop. After leaving the chamber she sat down and coughed and sneezed several times. Tears ran down her face. 'Not great, my throat is really irritated,' she gasped.

After a five-minute rest SG4 entered the chamber for the barbecue smoke test. It started normally but after thirty seconds the level of smoke seemed overwhelming. In fact, SG4 was not visible. Malinowski frantically panicked and pressed the remote continually without success in stopping the test. Cheng ran to the chamber and opened the door. SG4 almost fell out and Cheng guided her to the treatment bed. Both SG4 and Cheng coughed loudly. As SG4 laid down, it was clear that her nose was bleeding and blood was coming from her mouth.

CHAPTER 26

DAY TWENTY-SIX
MUSIC TEST

Wong and Cheng shuffled CDs in to four piles and looked at each other, smiling. 'This is gonna be fun,' said Wong.

'It will depend on people's tastes in music. If you don't like classical music, it would be difficult to know the difference between a trumpet and trombone,' said Cheng.

Wong laughed at that. 'Very good view, Asterina.'

The first patient to arrive was ML2. She looked relaxed and happy for the event to take place. Wong pointed to the patient's chair and ML2 sat down. Wont sat next to her and looked at his notes briefly. 'So, we are going to play some music and ask you to identify the different music instruments being played. We have four piles of CDs and they are numbered one to four. You need to pick a number and we will take a CD from that pile.'

'What are the four categories?'

Wong checked his notes. 'We have Country and Western, Chinese and Indian, General Pop, and finally Classical. So it's really pot luck. You choose a number, and we play a CD from that pile and you try and identify the instruments.'

ML2 crossed her legs and thought for a moment. 'I would like to choose number three please.'

Cheng lifted a CD from the top of the pile and said, 'You

have chosen Country and Western. 'Happy?'

'Not really,' said ML2. 'Not my thing, but what the hell,' she concluded. Cheng handed Wong the CD and he loaded it into the portable player. Cheng handed ML2 a small notepad and pen to write down the instruments. The track played and immediately ML2 started writing. After three minutes of listening, she had four instruments written down. ML2 handed the pad to Wong who briefly looked at it before handing it to Cheng. Cheng read out loud the instruments that ML2 had heard.

'Guitar, drums, violin, piano. You only missed bass guitar so well done.' ML2 rolled her eyes and sat up straight. Wong thanked her for her time and ML2 left the treatment room.

GB1 was the next patient to arrive and, after receiving instructions from Wong, she chose the number two pile. Cheng picked up a CD from pile two. 'You've chosen Classical, James Bond theme music,' she said.

GB1 put her head to one side and laughed. 'Great, I like a bit of 007 music.' Cheng handed the CD to Wong. Cheng gave GB1 the pad and pen to record the instruments. The music blasted out for several minutes. GB1 wrote down her thoughts continually and looked pleased at the end. She handed Wong her list who looked at it briefly and then handed it to Cheng for checking. 'So, what do we have here. Piano, lead guitar, bass guitar, drums, tambourine, trumpets, violin, very good. There were others like double bass, viola, well done. You can go now, have a nice day.'

SG1 arrived, and suffering from another coughing fit. He apologised profusely. 'No problem,' said Wong, 'that's why you are here.' Wong explained the procedure for the tests and then it was decision time for his patient to choose from which CD pile his test would be conducted. 'I'm not superstitious,' said SG1. 'So, I will go for number four and take whatever I get.'

Cheng took a CD from the fourth pile and gave it to Wong. Wong looked at the label and then looked at SG1. 'You've chosen Indian music; how do you feel about it?' SG1 shook his head from side to side and chuckled.

'Okay, I think I know a few instruments, so we'll see.' Wong turned on the music and it started slowly and gathered pace. Cheng realised she had not given the patient the pad and pen to write down his thoughts so quickly gave them to him as it was some way in.

'Do you want to start the music again?'

SG1 nodded. 'Let's do that.' Wong stopped the music and restarted. SG1 smiled widely as the sound of the sitar blasted out from the CD player. A few minutes passed and he wrote down a number of things on his pad. The music stopped and SG1 gave the pad and pen back to Cheng. Cheng checked the patient's notes. 'Sitar yes, hand drums yes, bansuri yes, alghoza (double flute) yes. There is one you didn't recognise. Er, the kuzhal. I think it's also known as a double reed. Well done.'

SG2 arrived ten minutes late and apologised to Wong and Cheng. Wong asked, 'What music do you like?'

SG2 thought for a few seconds. 'I like most kinds actually. Western pop music, canto pop, romantic songs from famous shows.' Wong told her the procedure and SG2 chose category four. Cheng gave Wong a CD from pile four and then gave the pad and paper to SG2.

'Write down any instruments you think you heard,' said Cheng.

Wong loaded the CD and said, 'You have got traditional

Chinese music, so good luck with your guesses.'

'Okay I look forward to it,' said SG2, looking happy. The music was played loud and SG2 quickly identified the guzhang (the string instrument), flute, and zheng. The music finished and Cheng checked the results. 'You found three, but you missed acoustic guitar, piano, and symbols.'

'Ah well that was an interesting experience,' said SG2.

SG5 arrived for his test carrying a large shopping bag. Cheng looked at it and inquired, 'Been shopping, have we?' SG5 took a large check jacket out of the bag and held it up. Wong felt the arm sleeve's texture.

'It's very smart.' SG5 put the jacket back and sat down in the patient's chair. Wong went through the procedure and SG5 quickly chose category two for his music. Cheng handed a CD to Wong and the pad and pen to SG5. 'You have got classical music so lots of instruments in there.'

'Great, bring it on' said SG5. The music played loud and then soft. SG5 wrote down furiously and the allocated time seemed to pass very quickly. Cheng took the pad from the patient.

'Right, let's see how well you did. Violin yes, piano yes, guitar yes, bass guitar yes, drums yes, double bass yes, very good. You missed clarinet and saxophone. Oh and a couple of percussion items.'

The next patient for the test was SG4. After being briefed by Wong, SG4 declared,. 'I'll go for number one. That is usually my lucky number.' Cheng looked at the piles of CDs remaining.

'Coming right up. You have chosen general pop music. Are you happy with that choice?'

SG4 chuckled. 'Yes, I am confident I will recognise a lot

from the music.' Cheng handed the CD to Wong and the pad and paper to SG4. Wong loaded the disc and it started with a piano softly and built up speed with guitars, violins, and trumpets. SG4 wrote down her answers quite quickly and when the music finished had a smile on her face. Cheng collected the pad from the patient and walked back to her workstation.

'Let's see how you have done,' she said. 'Piano yes, guitar yes, trumpets yes, tambourine yes, harp no I don't think so And there was an oboe you have not identified. So, you got most of them. Well done.'

Next patient was ML1, a successful restaurateur from Malaysia. Wong welcomed him to sit on the patient's seat and asked, 'How is your business doing?'

'Not too bad,' replied ML1. 'We are getting more tourists in JB these days.'

'Where are they from?'

'Actually, from all over. China, Hong Kong, Japan, and Europeans as well.' Wong went through the motions of the test and ML1 chose number one.

Cheng handed him a note pad and told him, 'General pop is your choice of music. How do you feel about it?'

'I am happy with it.' He smiled. Cheng gave Wong the disc and the music started. In no time the chosen piece of music was finished playing. Cheng took the notepad from the patient.

'So, what have we got. Acoustic guitar is correct, bass guitar yes, lead guitar and rhythm guitar yes, violin yes, Chinese gong yes, and various percussions and wind instruments is sort of right. Well done. Did you know that track, Bohemian Rhapsody by Queen?'

'Oh yes, love it,' said ML1.

The final patient for the music test was TW1, the Taiwanese student. After getting the run down from Wong she chose number four. Cheng gave TW1 the notepad and pen. Wong had a snag loading the CD and so asked Cheng for another CD instead. The second one was fine, and the music played. TW1 listened intensely and wrote down a few instruments. The music finished and TW1 gave Cheng the pad with her thoughts. Cheng checked the pad to the CD. 'Dizi yes, gugin yes, violin yes, guitar yes, tambourine yes, flute yes, drums yes. Well done, you recognized all of them.'

TW1 smiled widely at the result.

CHAPTER 27

DAY TWENTY-SEVEN
MK888 DRUGS ROBBERY

TW1 got out of the taxi and walked into terminal one. She was there to greet her three sisters who were arriving from Taiwan and staying in Singapore for a week's holiday. TW1 made her way to arrivals and looked at her watch. She looked at the board to see if her sister's flight had arrived. The flight had landed twenty minutes previous, so not long to wait she thought. TW1 read her emails on her phone while she waited for her sisters to arrive.

Fifteen minutes passed and TW1 could see her three siblings in the distance. They arrived, all giggling, Shu Ching, Annya, and Aliyah. Each one hugged TW1 in turn.

TW1 asked, 'Where are you staying?'

Annya replied quickly, 'Goodwood Park Hotel in Scott's road.' TW1 raised her eyebrows.

'Should be nice,' Aliyah chipped in. 'Shu Ching stayed there a few years ago so it was on her recommendation.'

Shu Ching commented, 'I like the outside pool and the restaurants are good.'

The taxi queue disappeared quite quickly. The four giggling girls got in the taxi and arrived at the hotel in no time. They hurriedly went into reception and checked in. After, TW1 suggested to her sisters that she should go to the restaurant and order food for all of them while they unpacked their suitcases. 'Any particular food you want?'

Shu Ching answered, 'We'll leave it up to you. Rice, beef noodles, a prawn dish. Just get a good selection and we'll add to it later.'

'Okay, don't be too long,' TW1 said.

TW1 walked to the main restaurant and asked for a table for four people and told the waiter that her three sisters would be joining her soon. After an initial drink order arrived, the waiter asked TW1 for the food order. 'Can I order food for four people? My three sisters are yet to arrive,' TW1 explained.

The waiter nodded his head. 'Okay, fine, I'll note that you don't want the food on the table for a little while. What do you want to order?' TW1 looked at the menu quickly.

'Alright could we have egg fried rice, beef noodles, prawns in garlic, duck and pancakes, chicken dou miow with chillies, bean curd with dried scallop …That's it.' The waiter wrote the order down and then smiled at TW1.

'What about drinks for your guests?'

TW1 thought for a second or two. 'Er just a bottle of still water and a bottle of Chablis.'

The waiter wrote the order and then said, 'We have two Chablis choices. Number eight is fifty dollars and number nineteen is one hundred and fifty dollars.'

TW1 smiled widely. 'Let's have the number nineteen.' The waiter disappeared and returned ten minutes later with the water and wine bottle in silver buckets.

TW1 typed a message on her phone to sister Annya, asking her to hurry up as she was feeling hungry. Annya immediately texted back. *Coming. Coming.* TW1 poured herself a small glass of the white wine and took a sip. A few minutes passed and the sisters joined her. The waiter appeared and stood at the table. 'Ready for your food now?' he asked.

Shu Ching gave the signal. 'Bring it on.'

'Anymore drinks for anyone?'

Annya put her hand up. 'Could I have a diet coke, please?'

'Coming right up,' the waiter replied.

Meanwhile, back at the hospital, a delivery van pulled up outside and the driver opened the rear doors but didn't take the drugs which were carefully packed in boxes out of the van. He walked into reception and spoke to Jenny. 'I have a few boxes of MK888 for you. Can I just use the toilet?' Jenny pointed the driver in the right direction. A few minutes later the driver returned to his van and went round the back to get the boxes out. In horror, he realised they were no longer there. He scratched his head and looked all around the front of the hospital. He quickly ran to the hospital entrance and looked both ways down Cairnhill Circle. There was no traffic in either direction. He quickly took his phone out of his pocket and called his office. 'Wei. Ni how. Charles here. I am at Singapore ENT hospital in Cairnhill. Here to deliver the boxes of MK888. I went inside the hospital reception and used the toilet. When I returned to my van the boxes had been stole ... Okay, I'll call the police and wait for them here ... Right will do.'

The driver phoned the police and reported the robbery. They told him it would be approximately thirty minutes before they could be at the scene. He walked into the reception of the hospital and explained to Jenny what had happened.

Jenny said sympathetically, 'How terrible, you were only away from the van a few minutes.'

'I know, I know,' said the driver, sweating profusely.

'Would you like a coffee or tea?' asked Jenny.

'Yes, I'd love a coffee with milk and no sugar please.' Jenny got up and walked to the coffee machine between her reception desk and made a coffee for the driver and one for herself.

Handing the coffee to the driver, Jenny said, 'There you go. You can wait here or, if you prefer, you can wait in the library. There is a TV room in there.'

'It's okay I will wait here and read the paper,' said the driver, picking up a newspaper and taking a sip of his coffee.

Twenty-five minutes later two policemen arrived and entered the hospital. Jenny showed the policeman and the driver into a side room where they could go through the event in private. The van driver joined the policeman and shortly after they were joined by Professor Lee. Lee asked the van driver to go through the events of the robbery and one of the policemen made notes on a pad. Lee held his head in his hands. 'I cannot believe this has happened,' he gasped.

The senior policeman asked, 'Do you have security cameras outside the hospital?'

Lee replied, 'Of course, we can look at that and find out what the thieves look like.' Lee picked up the phone in the room and dialled reception. 'Jenny, can you prepare the playback video of the time of the robbery and link it to the meeting room? ... Okay, thanks.' Lee turned to the policeman. 'I'll turn the TV on and we can see the robbery taking place.'

'That's very useful,' said the senior police officer. Lee got up from his seat and turned on the large TV that was fixed to a wall. After a few minutes a picture emerged. Then, after fiddling with the remote control, the picture became clear.

The van driver got out of the van and opened the back doors and then entered the hospital reception. After about half a minute two men appeared in a blue van and immediately got out. They quickly opened the back doors of the van then proceeded to the drugs' van and removed six cardboard boxes and carried them to their vehicle. Lee looked at the video intensely. 'Just a second,' said Lee, startled. He rewound the video and watched the robbery again. 'It looks like SG3 is one of the thieves.' Lee looked from the TV to the policeman. 'We had a patient here involved in a drugs trial and he discharged himself. He returned with a gun and then threatened me. There was an altercation and he fled.'

'Is that SG3 the guy in question?'

'That's him, little bastard,' snapped Lee.

The van driver shook his head. 'I am so sorry; this robbery is all my fault. I should not have left my van doors open, then the drugs could not have been stolen.' The others all looked at him but did not say anything. The video had gone past the whole robbery incident and now was showing a few people entering the hospital. The senior policeman looked at Lee.

'Do you think we could watch the video again from the start?'

'No problem.'

They watched the robbery again and at the end the senior policeman asked, 'You don't recognize the second thief?'

'No,' replied Lee, 'but the young guy with the coloured hair is definitely SG3. No doubt about that.' The senior policeman scratched his head.

'It's strange that SG3 appears just when a delivery of drugs arrived at the hospital. It's like he knew the delivery was going to happen. Weird. Okay, Professor Lee, that's all for now and we'll be in touch and hopefully the suspects will be found soon along with the six boxes of drugs. And thank you, driver, for your statement.'

CHAPTER 28

DAY TWENTY-EIGHT
NOSE AND THROAT EXAMINATIONS

The five members of the medical team sat at a round table in a meeting room. Professor Lee opened a large folder of notes and print outs. 'Is everyone alright?' he asked. 'Yes fine,' was the reply. Lee looked at his watch and then started his brief. 'Today we will conduct examinations of the nose and throat in our patients. The purpose of the meeting is to just go through the things we will be doing and looking for. Common problems with the nose or nos-related are – runny nose, sneezing, loss of smell, sinusitis, and snoring. Common problems with the throat are – coughing (with or without phlegm), nasal drip, temporary loss of voice, soreness and tonsillitis.'

Dr Malinowski looked at Lee. 'How long do you think we will spend with each patient on these examinations?'

'Well, if they go according to plan, it should be about an hour on each. But at times we will be working simultaneously. If we need more time, we will have to go into day twenty-nine morning. I have already cancelled a patient's appointment for tomorrow and you may have to do the same. Try to keep the morning free, if possible. In the afternoon I will expect us to do the weekly review for week four.' Lee took a large gulp of water and then continued.

'With each patient ask a little about allergies, occupation, operations, traumas, smoking, drinking, and pets at home. As with the inspection of the nose, you need to look at the nose from the front and side for any of these signs: size and shape, deformities, swelling, scars, crusting. Ask the patient to sniff in and out of each nostril while holding a finger to close the nostril and use an endoscope to view the nasopharynx. Inspect the roof of the mouth. Have a look for nasal polyps and tumours. These are more likely to appear in the soft palate rather than the hard palate.'

Tan asked Lee, 'Is it the case that mouth cancer is usually an ulcer without pain and then becomes painful later?'

Lee nodded his head. 'Yes, that is the usual situation. If the ulcer is not too large it is sometimes dealt with by radiotherapy only or maybe surgical removal.' Lee shuffled his notes. 'Okay so next I will go through the throat examinations and procedure. Right before examinations ask the patient about smoking and alcohol history. Then, when you examine, ask for dentures to be removed. Use a good bright torch. Nurse Cheng, will you check the stock of torches immediately after this meeting please?'

'Already done that,' said Cheng quickly.

'Well done,' smiled Lee. 'Right, carrying on then, we need to examine the mouth and look closely at the condition of the tongue. Next, look at the back of the tongue and tonsils. Touch the base of the tongue and look for tumours. Next thing is to inspect the uvula at the back of the throat. Examine the space between cheek and gums. After that we examine the floor of the mouth and look for duct stones and lumps. Also ask the patients to stick their tongue out. Take a fibreoptic nasopharynx. Any questions?'

Dr Malinowski raised her hand. 'Do we have a summary

of these requirements?'

Lee shuffled his notes. 'I have a printed copy for everyone here covering everything I just said. Also, when you next logon to your computer you will see an email from me of the same version.' Lee handed his four colleagues the patient notes. 'Right, we have about an hour before we start. Dr Malinowski has a meeting with a drug supplier so we will start this morning as follows: myself and Cheng will be conducting examinations in treatment room one and Wong and Tan will do the same in treatment room two. Malinowski will relieve one of us later. We'll see how it goes. I said earlier we may carry over to day twenty-nine, we'll see.'

The time passed quickly, and Lee and Cheng got organised for the first patient's arrival. Cheng picked up the phone and called treatment room two. 'Doctor Wong, Nurse Cheng here. Do you have a good supply of torches, nasendoscopies, etc.? … Yes, there are also some spares in the top left cupboard above the sink. Okay have fun. Bye.'

SG1 entered treatment room one and was welcomed by Lee and Cheng. He walked to the patient's chair and looked around, quite relaxed. 'Are you feeling good?' Lee asked.

SG1 smiled. 'I am in good shape.' Lee sat next to SG1 and pulled his chair nearer the patient.

'I'm going to closely look at your nose now. If you could just sit well back in the chair for me, thanks.' SG1 adjusted his seating position to suit the doctor.

'I have a pretty big nose,' laughed SG1.

'That's good,' said Lee. 'You can breathe more air.' They both laughed loudly, as did Cheng in the background. Lee changed to a serious face. 'I need some historical detail. Any breathing issues?'

'No,' replied SG1.

Lee continued. 'Never smoked?'

'That's right,' confirmed the patient.

'Any pets in the house?' Lee asked.

'A dog. No known allergies from that,' smiled SG1.

'Right let's take a look at your nose.' Lee looked closely from different angles, moving the patient's head from side to side. Lee took a tiny mirror device and placed it up each nostril in turn. Then he sat back in his chair. 'All looks good. Can you breathe in from each nostril in turn while holding a finger over the other nostril?' The patient did as asked. Lee thanked him and then asked, 'Could you now do the same breathing out?'

The examination continued.

'Right, now for the throat examination. Any issues in the past?'

'Only the coughing,' replied SG1.

Lee asked. 'Any alcohol use?'

'Yes, I do like a drink, but not in any great quantity. I don't remember the number, but I am slightly over the units guideline.'

'That's fine then,' said Lee, moving closer to the patient again. 'I will now inspect the mouth and throat.' Lee looked closely all round the tongue and mouth. 'Now I just need to look inside so I will use a nasendoscope through your nose. It shouldn't be too bad. Just a little discomfort for a minute or two.'

SG1 made himself more comfortable. 'I'm ready.' Lee carried out the procedure and concluded afterwards all was fine. The patient was given a nose spray to take away.

Meanwhile, in treatment room two, TW1 was in the chair

having a hot flush. Audrey Tan handed her a glass of water. 'Take that.'

TW1 said, 'Thanks, could I have a wet towel to wipe my forehead?'

'Of course,' replied Tan, walking quickly to the cupboard and removing a clean towel. She placed it under cold running water before taking it over to the patient. 'There you go.' TW1 covered her face entirely with the towel and after half a minute took it away.

'That's better,' she gasped.

Dr Wong walked over and asked. 'Are you happy to go through with the examination?'

'Yes, just felt a little hot-headed for a moment. Don't know why,' replied TW1. Wong looked at some notes and sat up close to TW1.

'Firstly, we will do a nose examination. Can I just ask a little about your medical history?'

'Fire away.'

Wong looked at the notes in his hand. 'You've never been a smoker?'

The patient answered quickly. 'That's correct.'

Wong continued, 'Any pet allergies, any nose-related issues apart from normal colds?'

'No to all,' replied TW1.

Wong nodded. 'Okay then I'll start the examinations.'

Tan handed Wong a long instrument that had a mirror at the end of it. 'I will just place this instrument at the base of your nostril to look inside.' The patient's eyes flicked wildly as she showed her nervousness. After a few minutes Wong gave the instrument back to Tan who exchanged it for a metal tongue compressor.

'Thanks,' said Wong. 'Is it cold?'

Tan replied, 'Yes, it's been in the fridge.'

Wong placed the compressor under the patient's nose and held it steady. 'Could you breathe out on to the compressor please?' The patient breathed out. 'Ah hah,' mumbled Wong. 'One nostril has exhaled less air than the other. Have you any catarrh in the nose currently?'

'No, I don't think so,' said TW1, surprised.

Wong sat back in his chair for a moment. 'No worries, we are giving all patients a nasal spray to use if they suffer from a blocked nose. Could you breathe in deeply?' TW1 did as asked.

Wong asked Tan to do the endoscopy. Tan sat close to the patient. 'I will place this long tube through your nose and down to the throat, arriving in your stomach. It's slightly uncomfortable but don't worry I will not hang around too long before removing the tube.'

'Okay fine,' said TW1, a little apprehensively. TW1 closed her eyes throughout the exercise and sneezed when it was over.

Tan gave the patient a moment to recover. 'Right, next we will take a look at the throat. Have you been a regular drinker of alcoholic drinks?'

TW1 smiled. 'Not much. An occasional glass of wine when dining out, nothing more really.' Tan picked up a torch and showed it to TW1.

'I will have a look around inside your mouth and tongue.' TW1 rolled her eyes and sat back in the chair.

Meanwhile, back in the treatment room one, Lee and Cheng had welcomed in their next patient – SG2. Lee pointed to the patient's chair. SG2 sat down and looked relaxed. 'How have you been getting on?' asked Lee.

'Quite well. But looking forward to going back to work after the stint here.'

'Remind me what is it you do?'

SG2 replied, 'I am an accountant for an accountancy practise in Tanjong Pager area.'

Lee looked at Cheng. 'Have you got everything ready?' Cheng carried a tray to the table near where Lee was sitting. Lee looked at the items on the tray and then referred to his notes.

Lee pulled his chair closer to the patient. 'You are here today to let us look at your nose and throat. Just to make sure everything looks in good order. Do you have any historical issues with your nose and throat?'

SG2 thought for a moment before speaking. 'Well just the coughing really, but I am frustrated because I have had an unexplained cough for around three years now. Cannot pin it down to anything particular. Since my stay at this hospital, and receiving MK888 daily, the cough has not improved or got worse. It's been the same throughout.'

'Let's take a look at your nose first.' Lee squeezed the patient's nose gently and looked at its appearance on both sides. 'Could you lift your chin up please?' Lee asked. 'Down again. Can you breathe in for a few seconds and then breathe out for a few seconds?' SG2 carried out the task and then sneezed. Cheng handed her a tissue. 'Lee picked up the compressor. 'I will hold the device below your nostrils and I would like you to breathe out through your nose please.' SG2 leant forward to carry out the task. Lee looked at the compressor and observed the condensation was the same from both nostrils.

'The next part is not too nice. I will place a tube in your

nose and put it down through your throat and down to your stomach,' Lee said seriously.

'Do you have to?' asked SG2.

'Yes, I am afraid so,' answered Lee. 'The endoscopy allows me to look at your throat, oesophagus, and stomach.'

'Okay let's get it over with.' Lee slowly inserted the tube into the patient's nose. She screwed her face up and a few tears ran down her face during the procedure.

'Are you alright?' Lee asked.

'I'll survive,' replied SG2.

After a little break Lee sat up close to the patient once again. 'Next I want to look in your mouth and have a good look around.'

'Be my guest,' said SG2 sarcastically. Five minutes passed and Lee smiled wildly.

'That's it. Well done, everything seems in order. I will give you a new nasal spray which will help if you get any cold-related problems. Also, it might be helpful against the drug's side effects.'

Back in treatment room two GB1 was small-talking with Tan. Wong was preparing the instruments required for examinations. Ten minutes passed and Wong was becoming frustrated with the two women gossiping. 'Can we make a start?' he snapped. Tan looked at Wong with a dirty, disappointing look.

'Alright, we'll start now.' Tan looked at GB1. 'Any previous surgery related to nose and throat?'

'No,' replied GB1.

Tan continued questioning, 'How many years have you been coughing?'

GB1 thought for a few moments, 'I think around five

years now.'

'Can you relate it to anything?'

'Not really,' replied GB1. 'However, when I was on the BER machine on day eighteen I did get a few red lights on the fruit analysis. Apples, bananas, oranges, blackcurrants, peaches, pears.'

'You forgot melon,' smiled Tan. They both laughed loudly. 'We'll start then, shall we?' Tan said, picking up the compressor. 'I will hold this device below your nostrils and ask you to breathe out of your nose on to it.'

'That's interesting,' remarked GB1.

Tan clarified. 'It's to check the condensation of each nostril to see if they are roughly the same.' GB1 put her head to one side, still a little puzzled. After that, Tan picked up the device with the mirror. 'I am going to just look inside your nose now with this little mirror.' Tan inspected the inside of the nose and followed that with a look at the shape and base of the nose.

Wong walked up to both of them. 'Should I do the endoscopy?' Tan looked at him with a smile.

'Would you?' GB1 got the jest that Tan didn't like doing the endoscopy. Wong did the endoscopy quite quickly and after he finished, he asked the patient what it was like.

'Not nice, ooh strange really,' GB1 replied. They both laughed mildly.

Wong carried out a thorough examination of the mouth and, when finished, concluded that everything was fine with the patient. Prior to leaving, Tan handed GB1 a nasal spray to take with her.

In treatment room one SG4 was settling in for her turn. Cheng asked her for an update. 'Not feeling that good, I am worried about my throat cancer. How that is gonna pan out?' Lee asked her about MK888. 'I don't think it has helped much so far. In recent weeks I think I have been coughing more,' she replied.

Lee pulled his chair closer. 'Are you okay to go ahead with the nose and throat examinations today?'

'Yes, I'll be alright.'

Lee continued. 'I need to ask, have you given up smoking since you found out you have cancer?'

'Yeah, I decided it may help so I quit. It's not easy. That nicotine is very addictive. Especially when you have smoked all your adult life. I am taking a few nicotine substitutes to reduce the anxiety.'

Lee thought for a moment and then made an anti-smoking comment, 'I suggest you don't take up the vape smoking idea. Not enough is known about the risks yet and it might come to light in the future that it is just as bad as normal smoking.' SG4 nodded in agreement.

Lee carried out the nose and throat examination and concluded that he could not find any additional problems with the patient. On completion, SG4 sneezed frequently. Cheng quickly handed her some tissues.

ML2 had arrived and was met by Tan and Malinowski (who had relieved Wong) in treatment room two. Malinowski asked ML2 about her work. 'My next assignment is in Seoul and Busan. I have a week's work modelling swimwear and a new range of linen trouser suits,' ML2 said with great excitement. Malinowski was impressed.

'That sounds very exciting. Have you been to South Korea before?'

'I have been to Seoul but not Busan so that will be a new

experience.'

Malinowski sat close to ML2 and read the standard pre-examination questions and briefed her on what was coming. Tan handed Malinowski the cold compressor and it was immediately placed under the patient's nostrils. 'Breathe on to the compressor please. Okay now take a little rest and breathe out again.' ML2 did the task and then coughed slightly. Malinowski took away the compressor. I think you may have a bit of catarrh in your right nostril as I observed less condensation from that one on the plate.'

'I see,' said ML2, shaking her head.

Malinowski continued, 'No worries, I will be giving you a nasal spray to take with you after the examination. This will work well when you get a blocked nose in the future.'

Malinowski got up from her seat. 'Dr Tan will now do an endoscopy. This will include placing a tube through your nose all the way past the throat and into the stomach. This is just to see if anything is unusual in there. Are you okay with that?'

'I don't fancy it but if it has to be done then it has to be done,' said ML2, making herself comfortable.

Tan sat close to the patient, holding the endoscopy. 'Here we go then. Just try to relax. It's not painful, just a bit awkward. I'll do it as quickly as I can.' Tan pushed the tube gently in to the patient's nose and all the way down to the stomach. After a minute she withdrew it ever so slowly in order to minimise discomfort. At the point of removal ML2 sneezed twice and Malinowski handed her a paper handkerchief.

After a short break Tan sat close to the patient. 'Could you stick your tongue out please? Now put your tongue to the left and then to the right. Okay relax.' ML2 blinked repeatedly. Tan continued the examination. 'I am just going to have a good look around your mouth. Try to relax while I do a little prodding here and there.' Tan finished the examination and concluded that all was well with the nose and throat of the patient. Malinowski placed a nasal spray in a small bag and gave it to ML2 as she was leaving the treatment room.

Across the way, SG5 held his hand on his bad hip as he sat in the chair. Lee asked, 'Still getting pain from the bad hip?'

'Yes, I am,' replied SG5 'The recent fall I had in the library has not helped. It set the pain off again.'

'Would he like a painkiller tablet?' Cheng asked.

'Thanks that might help.'

Lee got the equipment ready to use and turned to the patient. 'Are you waiting for a hip replacement op?'

'I am. There would appear to be a long waiting list for this kind of op.'

Lee sat close to SG5. 'I am now going to have a good look at your nose and also ask you to breathe on this device from your nose to see if both sides of the nose have the same breathing ability.' The test was carried out and the result was positive.

Lee allowed the patient a breather before carrying out the endoscopy. SG5 struggled with the examination. His eyes wept and his eyelids fluttered repeatedly through the examination. 'That was no fun,' SG5 complained. Lee looked at the patient seriously but said nothing.

In treatment room two Malinowski and Tan were anxiously awaiting the final patient. He was already fifteen minutes late. Suddenly, the door opened and ML1 staggered into the treatment room, laughing. 'Sorry, sorry I am late. I met up with a friend and time just passed so quickly.'

Malinowski asked angrily, 'Have you been drinking?'

ML1 smiled. 'I've had a few drinks.' 'What the hell!' Malinowski raised her voice. 'You know you are not supposed to drink alcohol while undergoing the experiment.'

'Oh dear,' said ML1 in a now more serious tone of voice. Malinowski threw a folder she was holding on to the desk.

'You can fuck off now. I am not inspecting a patient while under the influence of alcohol.'

ML1 staggered out and left the door slightly ajar. Malinowski walked quickly to the door and slammed it shut.

CHAPTER 29

DAY TWENTY-NINE
WEEK 4 REVIEW

The main meeting room was noisy with banter. All the medics were present and ready for the final review meeting. Professor Lee asked Dr Wong, 'Can you see who's missing?' Wong looked around the large table.

'Er, seven persons present and one person missing. Let me look down the list of patients.' Wong ticked off his list and then turned to Lee. 'It's the British lady, GB1. She is yet to arrive.' Lee looked around the room and then to Wong.

'Thanks, we'll give her another five minutes,'

Ten minutes passed and Lee shook his head, annoyed. 'There's always one, isn't there!' GB1 suddenly arrived and closed the door. 'Sorry Professor Lee, I got held up,' she said. Lee made no comment and waited for GB1 to sit down.

Lee got to his feet and welcomed everybody. 'So today is our last weekly review in our MK888 experiment. As usual I will be looking for people's experiences in the last week and any overall thoughts. Firstly, could I have a show of hands regarding bad dreams. I heard a rumour that patients were getting bad dreams in the last seven days. So, please anyone who had a bad dream in the last week raise their hands now please.' Every patient raised a hand. 'Well, that's is interesting. Okay I'll go around the table as usual.' Lee sat down and shuffled his papers.

'Can we a start with SG1 please. How have you found things in the past week?'

SG1 stood up and looked around the table at everyone and then fixed his gaze on Lee. 'Overall quite good, I think. I am definitely coughing less and feel that I may be cured soon. The little drama this week has been a bad dream. I had the same dream two nights running. It was about a big domestic cat chasing me around the house and looking as though it was going to bite me.'

'How fascinating,' said Lee, smiling. 'And did the cat actually attack you?'

SG1 laughed. 'No, I got away. But like most dreams it was pretty short time period.'

'Okay thanks for that,' Lee said. 'Now could I here from SG2 please?'

SG2 stood up. 'My week was without any improvement in my cough. Actually, so far, the MK888 has not helped my cough but hopefully further down the line it will do. This week I also had a peculiar dream. I dreamt I was trapped in a warehouse-type building, and I couldn't get out. Every door I tried was locked and it made me panic. Like SG1 it was short, but I awoke feeling a bit strange.'

Lee thanked her for the comments.

'Now SG4 your update please.'

'Still coughing bad, I don't know if MK888 has made it worse but then I have throat cancer so it may be that. The other thing is I am still suffering most days with stomach pain.'

Lee looked at Wong. 'Could you help SG4 with the medication?'

Wong said, 'Yes' to Lee and then looked at SG4. 'Sort you something out later.'

Lee looked at SG4. 'Can you tell us about your dream?'

'Oh yes. Not pleasant. I was driving a car through some woods late at night and the car's brake's wouldn't work. It seemed like the car was out of control and going faster and faster. I woke up feeling extremely stressed.'

SG4 sat down and SG5 got up. 'At the end of week three I had been sleeping better than the first two weeks. This was after a change of sleeping tablets. This week's sleeping is normal while still taking sleeping tablets. Coughing is still happening but is less week on week. As to my dream experience, it was weird. Very weird. I drove to a supermarket and did some shopping. When I returned to the car somebody had parked so close to my car that I couldn't open the door. Five minutes went by, and I began to get wound up. I should also point out that the other side of my car was near the trolley collection point with no space to get in the passenger's side. Anyway, I was to report my problem to customer services in the store when the driver arrived. I let him know that I wasn't happy and swore at him. He walked over to me and punched me in the face. I then punched him back and we had a fight. Result of which we were both quite bloodied and bruised.'

Next to report was ML1. 'My cough is slightly less prominent this past week. However, I have still been getting stomach-aches and wonder if I could have something different for that.'

Lee nodded. 'Dr Wong will sort out something different.'

'My bad dream was as follows: I needed some new spices for my kitchen and I thought I would take some from my restaurant next door, knowing that I had a very large stock of everything. It was around 11.30 in the evening. All the customers and staff had gone. I turned the lights on and slipped on a bit of grease on the floor. I lay on the floor in shock and in great pain. I was unable to get up from the floor and felt terrible. Then, fortunately, I woke up and realised it was just a bad dream.'

The next to report was ML2. After standing up she ruffled her short skirt down a little. 'Coughing is not too bad. I think since taking MK888 it has been a help. My nightmare dream was not very nice. I had gone to Hong Kong to appear in a fashion show. I was the last model on the catwalk and on returning to the dressing room all the others had finished for the day. Once I had changed from the modelling clothes into my own clothes I went for a little walk about in the storeroom. There were clothes everywhere and I noticed a door painted pink and yellow. I wondered what was in there so I went inside to have a look. It was full of ladies' coats. Bang, the door behind me closed and I noticed it did not have a handle. I rushed over quickly and could see that I had now got trapped with no way out. My stomach turned over and over. There did not appear to be a window or another door as I frantically searched the room.'

'So what happened, did you manage to get out?'

ML2 laughed, 'Well, I woke up sweating so that was the end of it.'

The next to report was GB1. 'Hi everybody, my situation is that I am making slow weekly progress. I still seem to get a bit of stomach-ache, but less. My cough is still present but not so bad.'

Lee asked, 'And did you have a bad dream in the past week?'

GB1 smiled meekly. 'Yes, I'm afraid so. My dream was

myself in New York. I wandered around Central Park on my own at night and felt very scared. There were very few people around and I kept walking and walking. I ended up in the north wood and it just seemed that I couldn't find a way out. Eventually feeling stressed and cold, I found a gate, opened it, and I was in Harlem area. It was quiet, apart from the odd car and taxi. Then I woke up. Mad! Strange.'

The final patient to report was TW1. 'Well, I must say I am pleased to report a cough-free week. I don't know if I am cured but hopefully that may be the case. I too had a nightmare experience this week. It was quite late at night, and I was walking to the train station in Orchard Road after an evening out with a friend. I thought I heard a humming noise from behind me in the distance. I looked behind me and was quite shocked to see a spaceship in the sky. It was cigar shaped and had many flashing lights. The strange thing was I was the only person to notice it. There were many people on the street, but they seemed oblivious to the strange thing in the sky. It was in the sky for only a short period before moving at great speed and it disappeared in the direction of Scott's Road.' Several laughs were heard from the other patients.

Dr Wong commented. 'That is a bizarre dream.'

Lee stood up. 'Thanks to everyone for today's catch up. And thanks for your participation in this drugs trial. Tomorrow we will have an exit appointment individually with you all. Then you will all go home. But you are invited back in three months to see how you have progressed. In that three-month period, you are free to contact the hospital at any time if you require any help or advice.'

CHAPTER 30

DAY THIRTY
CONCLUSION

Professor Lee stood at the entrance door of the hospital and watched the white delivery van arrive outside. The driver got out and immediately went round the back of the van and opened the doors. He then walked into the hospital with three boxes. 'Good morning, a new delivery of MK888.'

'Can you leave them on that seat by the reception desk?' Lee asked.

'Of course. Could you just sign the delivery note? Thank you sir.' Lee signed the note and the driver split the two copies, keeping one and giving the other to Lee. The driver left and Lee gave the delivery note to Jenny on reception.

'Could you phone Dr Malinowski immediately and tell her that the MK888 delivery has just arrived?' Jenny called Dr Malinowski and in less than two minutes she had arrived in reception.

'Take care of them!' Lec joked.

Malinowski picked them up. 'Don't worry, they'll be under armed guard ha ha!'

Lee went back to his office and read some emails on the computer. A recent email had arrived from Dr Audrey Tan. Lee had asked her to have a meeting with him about her experiences with the electric shock machine in South Korea. Lee picked up his phone and dialled. 'Audrey, would you be free now regarding our meeting on the electric shock machine? ... Okay see you in five minutes.'

Shortly after, Dr Tan burst into Lee's office carrying a large brown folder. 'Good morning, Benjamin.'

Lee smiled. 'Good morning, Audrey.' Tan sat down and opened her folder of notes and reports.

'To answer your questions, I have a number of reports here. In a thousand tests the following numbers of issues were reported. Ten suffered with depression. Five reported permanent headaches. Thirteen had temporary digestive problems – lasting less than one month. Three complained of a skin rash on the arms—'

The phone rang and Lee answered. 'Can I call you back in a while? I'm in a meeting with Dr Tan ... Okay. Thanks. Bye.'

Tan continued. 'Now, on the positive side, there are reports as follows: two cured of Parkinson's Disease, three with a cough of ten or more years stopped coughing, eleven had less muscular pain, and seventeen with heart problems were cured.' Tan flicked through the paperwork and read something. 'Not one patient died while in the electric shock machine in a small town in South Korea.'

'All interesting stuff,' said Lee, smiling. 'I do wonder about the accuracy though.'

Tan shook her head from side to side. 'Maybe.'

In the meeting room, exit interviews had started with Dr Wong and Dr Malinowski. SG4 was first to be seen. Wong asked sympathetically, 'Has your cancer treatment schedule been prepared yet?'

'Yes, I start the treatment in two weeks.'

Malinowski asked, 'And how are you feeling?'

SG4 rolled her eyes. 'Not great. The throat is feeling quite sore after the coughing. I don't have a problem swallowing food or drinks but at times there is a throbbing pain in the throat.'

'Are you going to be having chemotherapy and radiotherapy?'

'Yes. I believe high-strength radiotherapy daily and low-strength chemo daily. But not weekends. So, five days out of seven,' replied SG4.

Wong sighed. 'I am sorry. As time goes on it will get very tough for you. The radiotherapy is really hard to take after about two weeks. If it becomes too unbearable you will have to ask if they can lower the strength.'

'I am not looking forward to it,' SG4 said. There was a little period of silence. Wong took a large envelope off his desk and handed it to SG4.

'This is your exit pack. The contents are three months of MK888, a record sheet of anything you feel is connected to MK888, and some advice notes. If you need to contact us, feel free to do so at any time. Okay?'

SG4 took the envelope. 'Thanks so much.'

Malinowski gave SG4 a hug as she stood up. 'I hope everything goes well for you, and we will see you again in three months.' SG4 left the meeting room quickly.

After a ten-minute break Wong and Malinowski were joined by SG1. 'How's it been here for you?'

'Well, I think it's been a great success. I have not coughed much since taking MK888. It might be the case that I am virtually cured.' Wong and Malinowski looked at each other, smiling widely.

Malinowski turned her gaze to SG1. 'You will still take the MK888 for three months and return here to update us of your situation. We are giving you a supply of tablets for three months and various other reading matter.' Wong handed SG1 a large brown envelope. He thanked the doctor and left the meeting room.

The next patient to arrive was ML1, the sixty-year-old restaurateur. He coughed slightly after sitting down. 'Still coughing?' asked Wong.

'Not too bad. It is slightly better since taking MK888. At times I get a pain in the guts.'

'You have the new drug for that I prescribed yesterday?' Wong asked.

'Yes, I will give it a try with the next bout of stomach-ache.'

The fourth patient to arrive was SG2, the accounting lady. Greetings were exchanged. Wong asked, 'Have you enjoyed taking part in the experiment?'

'It's been fun, and I enjoyed the company of the other participants,' she replied.

'And has the MK888 helped reduce the coughing?' asked Malinowski. SG2 shook her head.

'Unfortunately, no. It has been about the same. The same for all four weeks.'

'Any side effects from the drug?' asked Malinowski.

'Nope, don't think the tablets have affected me like some of the others.' Wong handed SG2 the brown envelope and explained the contents and would see her in three months.

Dr Malinowski phoned Professor Lee from the meeting room. 'Benjamin, are you and Audrey still doing the remaining exit interviews? ... Okay I'll wait to you arrive.' Putting the phone down, Malinowski looked at Wong. 'Okay I'll wait for the others to arrive so you can go now if you want.'

Wong got up. 'See you later for the conclusion.'

Five minutes passed and Tan and Lee arrived, followed by SG5, the next patient for an exit review. Malinowski left the room and the meeting started. SG5 coughed three times and apologised.

Lee asked, 'How have you enjoyed your stay here?'

'I have enjoyed it. My cough is still present, but I suppose after twenty years it is going to take time. Even with a new super drug like MK888.'

'How's your sleeping now?' Tan asked.

'That's pretty good with the sleeping tablets you prescribed me,' replied SG5. Lee handed SG5 then big brown envelope and explained the same instructions as with the other patients.

ML2 arrived, as usual leaving a trail of expensive perfume in the air. Lee looked her up and down before speaking. 'How are you?'

'I'm good. Cannot say I enjoyed it that much being here. I'll be glad to get back to normal living.'

'Has your cough gotten better on this trial?' Tan queried. ML2 put her head to one side.

'Just a little. It's not gone yet but I guess I am coughing a bit less.' Lee picked up a large brown envelope and gave it to the patient.

'Take this with you. It contains MK888 for three months and a comment sheet. Let us know if you have any problems, otherwise see you in three months' time.'

'Thanks very much,' said ML2.

GB1 arrived for her exit interview in a bit of a flustered state. Lee asked what was wrong.

She replied, 'Oh, I need to get back working in the shop.

Since I've been away, I think things have gone to put. I just got a call from one of the staff and certain things that should have been done are not done.'

Lee smiled. 'Relax, enjoy your last day of freedom then.'

'Indeed,' agreed GB1.

Lee looked at his notes. 'I believe you've had a few side effects while taking MK888.'

'Yes, there have been a few headaches and stomach-ache along the way. As with regards to the coughing, it has been reduced a bit I'd say.'

Lee handed GB1 a large brown envelope. 'Here is your three-month supply of MK888 and a month's supply of tablets for the stomach pain. We will see you again in three months.'

'Thanks for everything.' GB1 said.

The final patient walked in. TW1, the young Taiwanese female student. 'Have you enjoyed your stay in Singapore?' Lee asked.

Surprised at his error, TW1 snapped, 'I live here. I am studying International Business.'

'Of course,' said Lee, rather embarrassed.

TW1 continued. 'I found this experiment interesting. And I think it may have cured my cough. For around a week now I don't think I have coughed once.'

'Very good,' commented Tan. Lee checked and read his notes. 'And the issues you had with stomach-aches, is it okay?'

'Yes, that has stopped.'

Lee gave TW1 her brown envelope of things to take with her and explained the contents.

Shortly after Lee left the meeting room and passed the reception on the way back to his office. Jenny, the receptionist, called him. 'Professor Lee, I have a special delivery from

Singapore General Hospital for you.' Lee took the large envelope from Jenny and walked quickly back to his office. He sat at his desk and opened the drawer to get a paper knife. Frantically he opened the envelope and removed its contents. Lee looked through the papers quickly and he anxiously wanted to know the contents. It was the autopsy report for HK1. 'Oh my god,' he shouted out loud. Nervously, Lee picked up the phone and dialled Malinowski. 'Malinowski, can you drop everything and come to my office now please?' He put the phone down aggressively. Malinowski burst into Lee's office not long after the desperate call.

'What's so urgent then?' Lee looked depressed and gave the autopsy report to Malinowski.

'It's the autopsy report for HK1. We need to read it and put it down and read it again several times. I did spot a reference to an unknown substance in the stomach.'

Malinowski slowly sat down in a chair while reading through the report. After a few minutes she looked up at Lee. 'So, the cause of death is Stemi heart attack, which is the worst heart attack you can have. There were problems with the lungs caused by smoking and the liver had cirrhosis.'

Lee looked at Malinowski intensely. 'And what about the stomach, read the section on Gastrointestinal System.' Malinowski flicked through the various pages and eventually found the section Lee referred to. She read the details out loud.

'The oesophagus and stomach are normal in appearance without evidence of ulcers. The pancreas shows evidence of autolysis and an unknown subsistence that has created two legions. Well, what is it?'

Lee shook his head from side to side. 'That is the sixty-four-million-dollar question. An unwelcome substance that has caused two legions.'

Malinowski raided her eyebrows. 'That could be our MK888.'

'That's what I am thinking,' Lee agreed. Lee looked at his computer and then back to Malinowski. 'Before I forget, did you look into previous studies on dreams caused by new drugs?'

'No, I haven't yet. I think I may have something from the past. A slimming tablet tried in Switzerland reported dream issues in 2014. I just need to locate the info.'

Later in the day, all the medical team met up in the meeting room for a conclusion meeting. Professor Lee, Dr Tan, Dr Wong, Dr Malinowski, and Nurse Cheng sat round the table. Lee looked at a few notes he prepared and then spoke. 'Here we are then at our conclusion meeting. What do we conclude about the results of our MK888 drugs trial? Dr Wong, would you like to give us your thoughts on the last month?'

'I enjoyed it a lot. All the tests we did and the range of people and the backgrounds they came from made it fun. Give me a second to try and recall anything not previously reported. Oh yes, I suppose the most colourful characters out of all our patients was HK1. On one occasion I had been having a night out in Orchard Road and was driving home when I noticed HK1 staggering down the road drunk. No doubt he had a drinking problem. I have a friend, Harry Choo, who owns a bar in the Orchard area. Harry came to see me about 10 days after HK1 had died. Apparently, HK1 had been a customer of Harry's bar and not paid for a couple of night's debauchery. Harry didn't know HK1 had died of a heart attack but wanted me to try and get the money for the unpaid drinks, etc. I told him that it was unlikely we could do that.'

Lee chipped in, 'Well we are not going to pay the bar bill from the hospital. Nor will I ask Jasmin, HK1's wife, because I know she'll bite my head off.' Lee shook his head wildly. 'Okay let's have the thoughts of Dr Malinowski.'

Malinowski smiled wildly. 'I think it's gone well. A few issues here and there. The headaches are sometimes evident of a new drug. But dreams and stomach pain are a bit of a concern.'

'Yes, it's the stomach pain I am worried about. HK1's autopsy report has reference to an unknown substance found in the stomach. The cause of the legions they think.'

Malinowski continued, 'Hopefully MK888 is not the cause of long-term stomach issues otherwise that could put in doubt its marketability. It seems all new drugs affect patients initially and then go away. Our drugs trial of ten patients is very small. If it were 10,000 it might be a different conclusion.

Lee looked at Nurse Cheng. 'Asterina, what were your highlights and concerns in this experiment?'

'Er I had a problem getting a pulse with SG5, our retired schoolteacher. Yes, a number of times that I had to delay his blood test to another day because I couldn't get a sample.'

'Interesting, did he have high blood pressure?' asked Malinowski.

'Yes, I think so,' replied Cheng. 'Then again, with SG5 he had a bad experience with the smoke chamber test. His face went as red as beetroot, and he had a bad cough for some time after. I felt so sad for SG4 getting diagnosed with throat cancer, must have been a hammer blow!'

Lee sat back in his chair. 'I think she may be fine as it's not got to the advanced stage. And Dr Tan, what are your thoughts of the last thirty days?'

'To be honest, I am a bit knackered. It has been very stressful but a great experience. Obviously, the most interesting and worrying patient was SG3. It was unfortunate he suffered so badly after the electric shock test. As you know, I had some considerable experience of this machine in South Korea. Most of the tests were okay. Patients didn't suffer too many side effects. Of course, we don't know the mental state of SG3 before he joined our trial. Some of the kids may be taking drugs these days. And the incident with the gun and a second return to the hospital to steal the delivery of MK888 tablets. Shocking!' said Tan.

Lee had a worried look on his face. 'Yes, and he's still out there, the police cannot find him.'

ABOUT THE AUTHOR

Stephen Ball is a retired accountant, now author.

MK888 is his first book. Born in Newmarket, Suffolk, UK, he worked in Cambridge, London, China, and Singapore.

His interests include watching sport and cooking foreign food.

Future projects include an *MK888* film based on the book and a children's book and animated film.

Printed in Great Britain
by Amazon